verses of forgiveness

Myriam Antaki

verses of forgiveness

A NOVEL

Translated from the French
by Marjolijn de Jager

OTHER

Other Press • New York

Copyright © Actes Sud, 1999
Originally titled *Les Versets du Pardon*

English language copyright © 2002 Other Press

Production Editor: Robert D. Hack

This book was set in Electra by Terry Berkowitz, New York, NY.
Design: Terry Berkowitz

10 9 8 7 6 5 4 3 2 1

Cet ouvrage, publié dans le cadre d'un programme d'aide à la
publication, bénéficie du soutien du Ministère des Affaires étrangères
et du Service Culturel de l'Ambassade de France aux Etats-Unis.

This work, published as part of an aid program for publication, received
support from the French Ministry of Foreign Affairs and the Cultural
Services of the French Embassy in the United States.

Library of Congress Cataloging-in-Publication Data

Antaki, Myriam.
  [Versets du pardon. English]
  Verses of forgiveness / Myriam Antaki ; translated by Marjolijn de Jager.
    p. cm.
  ISBN 1-59051-038-0
    1. Terrorists–Palestine–Fiction. I. De Jager, Marjolijn. II. Title

PQ2661.N665 V4713 2002
843'.914—dc21

                                                        2002029348

The translation of this novel is dedicated to my
three grandchildren, Caleb, Stella, and Luca,
who are already blessed with the love of their parents.
May their lives also be guided by peace and forgiveness.

Darkness should never be a reason not to see the light.

— Auguste Valentin

part one

the terrorist of palestine

I AM A TERRORIST, A DREAMER. I have removed my mask of bliss for that of fear and sweat. I have lost. Some call me a hero, others curse me, but I have chosen my own image, my own identity, for I was soft wax that had to harden, inexorably.

My name is Ahmed but my father and mother never named me so. Born from an accident of love, of fate, I come from a legend in which their two lives were sealed by a vehement love and a long, slow absence without the relief of oblivion. I come from the depths of night, for when a man and a woman tear each other apart it is always night.

The light shining on my face, the face of the abandoned child, the wild orphan, is also the light of the paths of dream, war, and truth.

I have been hiding from the light but now it flows

into the half-darkness of my cell, which smells of mildew and rot. I look at myself in this light. My fingers bleed, my body bleeds. I am bespattered as a Caesar wearing his triumphal toga. The uprooted do not like to go through life in silence. I have atoned, the final hour of my fate draws near.

I am a terrorist but also the passerby who hides the dream's effrontery inside — daytime I watch the wingless clouds of blue, at night I love the shooting stars as they disappear into the folds of the sea. All alone one night, I chose one that had fallen from an unfamiliar sky and called her Iman.

I think of you tonight, Iman, and go back in time to hold you one last moment. You are the most beautiful of the girls in the Baalbek brothel and I have shared you with so many others. The memory of you is a story of rapture, a genie escaping from a lantern that burns.

For you I leave my camp, forgotten beneath a blistering sun, where all I learn of life is days of bitterness to come. There I forget love's slightest gesture, for it has never been granted me.

Iman, I dream of you, your olive skin, your haloed breasts, your mysterious navel, and your lips swelling with desire... Forgive me, I cannot change my way of thinking despite your body and your pleasure. Do not forget me, it is easier to remember someone who is dead than someone alive who loves another. I am taking our night cries with me. Some believe in eternal happiness, others wonder whether it exists and yet they always talk about it. A story hidden, one might say.

Iman, my tale is ending at last. The world's resplendent threshold belongs to others, those passing by. My life will end as dreams and seasons, winds and tempests end. I was created for disaster by a fluke. Fatherless, motherless, and homeless with a thirst for love that flings me like an aged child into the nakedness of the world. I have often dreamed that I was dead so that my parents would die with me and I could recognize and touch them.

Childhood is beyond repair and its wounds are always festering. Its suffering hurts in half-hearted concern. I have few memories. Born on the edge of a vanishing road, I was tossed at the door of a camp of Palestinian refugees, where tents stop under an invisible air of silence escaping from death. That lost and forgotten place is called Nahr al-Bared, the chilly river. A white-bearded sheik took me in to give me the name Ahmed and to create my face. He abandoned me in an orphanage the color of dry stone and dead ivy. Thus I was born and grew up in Lebanon, on soil not mine. In this welcoming land I released my pain and discovered the other shore, the one that led nowhere. Tonight, from the depths of my sorrow, I see Lebanon again, the naked foam of its waves. It is fading in the haze of a painless sun.

I am with you, Iman, it is the last time. I am wrenching you away from life, from oblivion, I tear you apart, I love you. I want to take your reflection with me. There are beings who are made to age, others who are dying from the start, and you, you are so young. Farewell, Iman. Your dark eyes immersed in ivory have a mystical beauty, your lips are painted in words of prayer. You are such an innocent creature and we loved each other so between those stained and yellowed sheets, like two birds embracing each other in a crystal cage in order to see the light.

I know, Iman, that you are a servant by nature, but so alive in giving me a rose or bringing me a drink. With you, I am the man who discovers hidden stars. You do not know that dawn belongs to another face of mine, a face that loves the world's diabolic ugliness, violence, the smell of death. And yet, dawn has eternity's most beautiful color, it is pink and comes out of the night. I, too, come out of the night and I am afraid of my memories. A forbidden child, I play beneath weeping clouds, I writhe and ripen in my orphanage in Lebanon. My tears are old, my voice is breaking, I think I am a yellowing leaf, my life is a fusion of fear and revolt. Suddenly a sheik emerges in the budding dawn. He is the one who took me in, I owe him my life. His gigantic, early morning shadow moves toward me. I never could give a name to that sorcerer's apprentice who speaks to me with untamed melancholy. He teaches me to avenge my land, my mother, myself, Palestine's son, disinherited by destiny. I listen to him. My heart opens up, the sun is metallic and hard, I exist at last. The unknown man vanishes in the lingering light. I graft a learned and vital image to my heart where violence lays anchor and crystallizes. I wait for night to come, a slow cold night, the true accomplice of loneliness, to flee the orphanage and slide like lava into a camp of terror. The darkness is dense, the moon a shining sliver over Baalbek.

Iman, forgive me, I have never reflected on my actions. On the edge of the abyss, I am discovering the mysterious appeal of having reached the end. Iman, keep my desire, my breath for yourself, I am still dreaming of love. My departed ashes will be incense.

One night, a gray and sorrowful woman finds me at last, with you. Her face is as pale as a communion wafer and her gaze is staring, like an icon's eyes. Her dress is black, as is her life. She has grown old for having long sought me in camps submerged in mud and dust. She reads tombstones covered with unfamiliar names and finally finds me in a house where love is sold. Remorse sheds a pitiless eye on her. She says:

"My son, I am your mother."

My mother finds me at last, in your arms, Iman, a man passing through, haunted by exploded dreams. I am already on the fading road and in my gaze, in yours, there is the profound certainty I shall leave you to go and die. That, too, is a way of loving. You have been a passage, a tunnel of pleasure toward love. You make me laugh, Iman, naked you are beautiful, your body the color of flames.

Mother, you meet me late, so very late, I have but a few days left, snatched from the past, the future I present to Iman forever. You are trembling and kneel down close to me. Your eyes caress me. Iman weeps, she listens to you filled with tenderness. Mother, your hands are blue with parched veins and sadness, you are old from suffering, from dying each day to live each day. Your hands clasp mine so strongly, stronger than in prayer. For you I am a distant silhouette who grows up in voiceless suffering despite the world's silence. Your words are from an era that flees and returns. You give me the journal my father wrote to offer himself to you or to find shelter in an elsewhere that belongs to you. Yet, you keep his name, his face from me, memories are greater dead than alive. There is your letter, too, the one you spent your life writing to him to declare your heart, find your words, and deep within yourself hide a truth you lost, the truth of love.

Mother, you move away again beneath the white, pale sky, and our invisible, thwarted bonds bring me to your honed, heart-rending happiness despite myself. You are a nocturnal butterfly that burns its wings to touch the light and disappears to weep. I keep the fine woman's handwriting that is yours on me, and the journal of a father I do not know. I dare not embark upon the reading and yet crave your words hidden in ultimate oblivion... Liberating your words, seizing my inception, my life from their secrets, their taboos, is to risk making myself vulnerable and frail. I am afraid to read your lives that preceded mine and thus to destroy my violence that liberates the world. This deep and secret past may appease my rage, squeeze it into an imaginary bubble of frozen mist. I am a terrorist and without the hatred that disfigures me my life would be stale and dull, a fleeting illusion....

I, Ahmed, come from nowhere and seek the paradise that is lost on roads that are lost. To overpower people I must place my explosives in the heart of a land where milk and honey flow. It is in violence that just once I touch my land, my land of Palestine. I leave my camp engulfed in light as slow as a sad morning.

Darkness passes and its immense black wings hide the fear, the silence. With my fingers, my hands, I touch the explosives around my waist the way a mourner kisses a coffin of death. I have a strange, supremely sensual dream in which a belly dancer attaches a string of pearls around her loins.

My explosives mutilate mothers, children, voiceless things. There is an intense flash that blinds howling fathers and animals collapsing. All those who are dead were waiting for life with its scent of burning perfume, incense, and light. I see their look again staring at the accursed dream. I do not bemoan their agony, it is so small compared to mine. With them, I drown the world's despair, my own, at the bottom of a precipice of stones and mud.

The rain is falling everywhere in spite of me. It moistens their blood with holy water and washes my face without cleansing my conscience or my hands. This evening, in my jail, I hear it still like a sad song rocking a sick child. The rain and smell of humid earth are my freedom's last fragrance.

I am a terrorist, a dreamer, I live love's cruelty. Now the walls close over me and trace scars that time incriminates. Torture has consumed my body, my dream, my breath comes slow and heavy. All is done. I am a condemned man, my hatred is dead, extinguished. My last wish is for my roots to be the future.

At last, I open my father's pages, my mother's pages, and read this distant past so that my soul may be born. In these forgotten sheets of paper I find my solitude again. We write in the illusion of discovering ourselves, of being real just once before we disappear. My eyes are burning, they see a garland of joy, dancing and tormented. I touch immovable time in order to understand it and to record my life in a confession of peace.

Father, mother, come into my blank paper, for I, I am leaving with the light. Come and love me just this once. I am writing you, happy people never write. I read, I learn, I hold on to your laughter, your dissolution, and carry you with me into the world of shadows. It is the magic of writing that invents futures, pasts, or oblivion perhaps. Father, in decoding your journal I find myself an identity by which your blood flows into me. Mother, I picture you through your letter and slowly melt into the hollow of your tenderness. I was born of your forbidden love that, for me, is not a flaw but a moon of expectation. I must pay and die.

I, Ahmed, son of the Koran, I am the terrorist of Palestine. My unfulfilled writing is the mute vision of a condemned man embracing a bit of happiness at last. I have gone to the very end of life despite pain, I have wept, and I have dreamed.

Father, mother, in blackened pages I come upon you, across a dust of haziness and stars. I am writing you a story of love, your story and mine, in order to exist, to touch you, to disappear. Written for you, my last words are verses of forgiveness.

part two

verses of forgiveness

*F*ATHER, THESE WORDS ARE THE REMEMBRANCE of days we did not have together. We could have taken walks along the beaches of Cordouan to watch the light fade into the ocean. The sand would have kept the traces of our steps beneath the rush of sleeping stars. You would have taken my hand to tell me the story of a siren or a sea monster when the wind was blowing the water's foam over the Atlantic. The wind, though, has scattered our lives beneath other sunless suns, a frenzy of distance and destiny.

Father, how could I ever have imagined that you came from France, the West, which for me has only the color of distant soil, of an infinitely low sky. I picture your blue eyes gazing at a lush, unfamiliar place and unravel your connections to an elsewhere in luminous mystery, a worldly origin.

You are the child of Cordouan, running on the banks to touch the mist flying off like slow smoke. You are going to your hiding place between two rocks, the stone shaped like a seat. This is your refuge, your look-out post, and this is where you discover life in the colors of waves, sky, clouds, and stars.

They call you the solitary child of the sea. The Atlantic is gray, the town behind you shines high up into the clouds. The streets leave paths, footprints on the piers, and shop windows tell their stories to the very youngest ones. You stand still, your heart brims over, happiness is complete.

Trees and the wind's murmurings surround your house. The brook ripples its water with a clicking sound you no longer hear. The flowers on the rosebush are translucent. Huge wings are cooing in the dove-cote. His name is Solomon, hers Salome. His head is crowned with feathers, her eyes are full of tenderness. You throw them seeds and hold them in your hands. They both fly off and then come back to you. In the distance you hear the lovely voice of your mother's music. Light moves around her.

Shimmering on the sea and in the clouds, the dawn takes on a color of silence. You are in your bed and dream of glowworms hiding in the plants on nights when it doesn't rain. You think they are star droplets.

Your mother bends down to kiss you and her hair covers your shoulders. She has the most beautiful hair in Cordouan, locks tinged with fire. Your mother is doing her hair, you are close to her and touch her long tresses with your fingertips.

Outside the ocean is carrying off its ships. You would like to be that dreamer, that student of poetry, a sea captain who leaves and on a distant island finds another woman who resembles your mother and offers you a similar scent. On the table the roses from the garden are wilting in a vase. The wooden floor is bare, the furniture simple. Light filters through the lace curtains.

The water in the harbor is calm. The road to school runs along the beach. The book bag on your back is heavy. Cars, either gray or black, go by. Out of habit you avoid the tramp with his dirty fingernails. He throws his cigarette butts away and soils the sea. The skin on half of his face is red and wrinkled. He wouldn't be such a monster if he would smile just once at the child, the passerby. This morning he is sitting in a corner slowly stroking a white cat. On the fur his hands are black. You move toward him, hesitate, but you do like white cats. Suddenly the man, his eyes shining triumphantly, pulls out a stick and slaughters the cat. His laughter is devastating to your eyes and ears. You flee, you want to codify life and wonder why God allows little cats to suffer. Perhaps pain can be hidden in a matchbox deep inside a drawer. Anxiety haunts your child's dreams.

Your father, a silent man, teaches at the school of education. His profession, in which discipline is the final arbiter, has desiccated him. In the evening he devours all that he can read. For you he is all-powerful and rules over the minds of his students, your mother's beauty, and your child's heart. The pots glean the golden reflections of your home. The night is filled with light.

Father, you love the whirling of the ocean, the foam, the waves. In Cordouan, the sea is blonde. Between the rocks and their shadows you choose golden shells, one at a time. You make designs with them on the moist sand or throw them down haphazardly to read the future. You keep them carefully at the bottom of a metal box and on its cover you write "My little friends."

In the summer, the water becomes blue. You are going to Floirac. Your mother packs two suitcases for the three of you. Your father puts his books in a carryall to prepare his courses in eternity's garden as he calls it. The sun is colored pink, shining on this recess of earth where summers are mellow. For you, every flower has the exquisite beauty of a liquid scent, of dew. Birds sing of happiness, the hours go by in sweet intoxication.

Father, you are big now. You no longer want to imbue gray smoke with the colors of the rainbow and you know that fairies exist only in stories. Your face is pimply, your parents are near you like a world possession and a gentle regret.

All three of you are in the sun in Floirac but a storm of destruction is already swooping down over the summer, the bare trees of winter. The war snatches memory away from the past and parades its deadly ghosts. To all of you it seems so far away.

One morning you are reading in the shade of the linden trees. The light is soft, your father comes over and sits down on the same bench. You push your books aside to make room for him, he smokes his pipe, biting it. He talks to you about this and that, he knows your resolute and assertive intelligence. He has never praised you, but you remember the conversation from beginning to end, in which you were the same age, had the same smile. The linden trees seem to protect the paroxysm of affection that binds you and keeps you close to each other under their leaves and in their shade. Then your father speaks these words to you: "Life is confusing, my son, but in love, in awareness, in God, there is always something to give."

The summer passes, you leave Floirac. The lindens

are deeply saddened. I see you, Father, in Floirac, in Cordouan again, near the magnolia trees, the flowers, the sea. Throughout my life, I have been a bit of a madman in exile, searching for a piece of garden… Like you, I am active by nature, instinctively, emotionally, burning with dreams and desire.

The time to be happy is short. Happiness is an avowal that vanishes as soon as it is repeated. It is the image of a man awake but dreaming, closing his eyes so he won't see anything anymore. There are paradises that disappear with lost childhood, with dreams, with suffering. The war trots out its procession of hate. It moves on like an evil fairy with her sinister laugh, her eyes wounded by fire and death.

The German army enters Cordouan. The ocean is lit up beneath the moon and repeats its sad song like a stifled passion. The army enters Cordouan. The sea is blue and sad. Adolescents parading. With chests pushed out, all of them wearing the same blue berets, they repeat the chants that seem to have lost their patriotism, music, and devotion. The official demonstrations have betrayal as their only justification. Failure and humiliation are based on a mystique of hope.

There are not many Jews in your town, but your name is David, I cannot believe it. The joy of finding you and then suddenly losing you, obliterating you. Father, you are a Jew! It is you whom I deny and assassinate. Life's effrontery produces buried mysteries, trembling and shouting voices. I am afraid of the truth, it sometimes delineates accursed and irreparable destinies.

There are not many Jews in Cordouan, but you all wear the yellow star as a sign of disgrace. That way they recognize and avoid you in those dark times of history. Uppercrust families play bridge and go hunting with the German officers. Women grab lovers in their flattering uniforms, who whisper strange words to speak of love. The sound of the waves breaks on the ramparts. The moon trembles in the water's tides. The Gestapo's black cars go back and forth through Cordouan, and Von Postel reinforces his positions. He is tall and handsome but nothing, neither hate nor remorse, brings any color to his eyes. He disengages himself from those masses of men who play roles that are too unwieldy for them, but hang on to them to call a halt to their own vacuity.

Your father disappears into the night and your mother hides in the dark of the curfew as if darkness could encircle rapture, salvage light. When you come home, her head is buried under her huge mass of hair, the only luxury of warmth and beauty. Many silences separate you, but one evening she raises her eyes to you, the candle melting close by her, and says: "David, you are old enough to leave, but a mother is a harbor, don't forget that."

The music has been cut off, the radio station shut down so that the discordant voices, the criminal feats, the arrogant tirades sullied with blood will not be heard. Persecutions and death surround the happiness of the Jews the way the sea surrounds an atoll with its stormy waves. Rain falls. This night your father lies down next to your mother in the double bed you find so narrow. You are happy he is there and almost forget the war. Your parents are talking very quietly, words and silences you can barely guess at. You dream of a shimmering ship on the water carrying things away and vanishing where the sea ends. The sound of the water scrapes at the tiles. They are ugly with the paper glued on for the blackout. It seems that light attracts misfortune. You doze off and dream of being a child sitting on your mother's lap to play with the beads of her long necklace. Your cheeks touch as in a Greek icon. Suddenly your mother is dressed in black, her hair is short and red, her face bony. You are afraid of her and cry out. It is dawn, the doorbell rings.

It is not the milkman's time. It is dark. The night is claiming its last glints of gray. Anxiety claws at you, you foresee disaster. The sound of the doorbell resembles a blade slicing through bliss. The Gestapo's black car jams on the brakes. The doorbell rings, long and insistent. Your father gets up. He takes his first steps toward the door, toward loneliness. He opens up, his robe is brown, his face homely with fear.

The policemen give him time to get dressed, a final

courtesy before his slow march toward death. He puts on heavy clothes and glances at the unmade bed, the faded roses, he knows he will never see Sarah — your mother— again to embrace her or possess her between these white sheets in which he would hear her breathing as she slept. He thinks of you but has a more difficult time tearing himself away from her, for she is a sensuality he has come to know, a love that belongs to him. He cannot even caress her hair one last time and barely dares to glance at you or her. You do not know whether he has any thoughts of contrition or of a hero's courage but in his velvet and fear-filled eyes you read the whole world's tenderness.

The door closes again, the Gestapo's car speeds away in a loud, victorious roar. You lower your eyes and cry: "Goodbye Father!" The day breaks over Cordouan, the sea is calm, smooth, silent. You don't go to class and stay close to your mother. She doesn't weep, looks elsewhere, at the white of the clouds. She already belongs to a world of shadows and silence as if she had to follow your father on the same path forged with their hands and dreams. You give her something to drink, a drop of wine, you peel a boiled potato for her, and make her lie down on the couch close to the fireplace. The fire is dwindling, smothered. You go out into the night.

The stars are shimmering with eternal light. Your rock is waiting for you and the sea becomes a stormy blue. Deep inside you there is a bottomless gash, for your innocence belongs to the past, to memories buried and lost. You know that between existence and happiness there are pages blank with a ghastly whiteness. A few clouds blot the stars. You open your box of shells, your "little friends," and throw them into the sea so they may be reborn in a more beautiful world. You watch them disappear, the water swallows up dreams and oblivion. It is your farewell to childhood, to adolescence. Rain falls in superfluous sadness.

The Free French and the British want to know what is happening in the Atlantic ports. Cordouan has remained mute on beaches desolate with weariness. Somewhere a transmitter is needed for a radio connection with Perigueux broadcasting to London. The war continues vigorously, intensifying and abating in death and blood. Racism becomes a religion, and what is human is lost at the bottom of the abyss. France cannot wait any longer, the Vichy policy is not justifiable anymore. They must fight even if the mind's morale does not join in with that of history.

The School of Education continues to be the center of agitation. The seed doesn't die, it takes root and germinates. On the pier of Cordouan a German sentry lies in a pool of blood whipped by the salt water of the sea.

A crisis turns life in Cordouan upside down. A German sentry has been assassinated on the pier of the harbor. That is where you dream of strange ships sailing beneath the white clouds you call siren's hair. A patrol of the Gestapo is hunting down the attackers. They are young and of the age to deserve being with God or to believe in mankind until the bitter end. They arrest just one. His name is Rémy, he has a blond lock that covers his forehead, his face. Perhaps he dreamed the wrong dream but he is your father's student. His crime is a mystique of anxiety, of humiliation. He has two accomplices who, like him, lie in wait and kill surreptitiously.

Von Postel receives the teacher and the student. The dark hallways smell like a sepulcher. Fear sows an odor of entrails in the cells' walls. The German's eyes are wide with anger, he demands names but wants to appear human. Men are resistant to long interrogations. For your father, revolt is his last ecstasy of life, a force by which to accept death. Rémy, though, has visions of dawn, of pale light. He is afraid and wants to be reconciled with his lost innocence. He loves life.

How long does the torture go on, how long does a man go on? There is no paradise where hate and mercy meet, all that remains is the shame of winning at any price. The waves ripple on the beaches beneath pallid moons. Night settles in like day in Cordouan's recesses under veils of solitude, shrouds of death. Your father dies under the torture. Von Postel sees his face covered in sweat and blood again when the hour strikes in which he watches the burning fires, the burning ashes. A screen of red haze comes before his eyes. You cannot cover the death of others with paint, but a dead conscience is daubed with triumph.

Rémy is afraid. A dark energy distances him from the heroic feat and binds him instinctively to life. He betrays his friends but does not yet know that the doors of misfortune are heavy and hard to close again. He lingers in the streets and no longer loves the sun. Fog cloaks him like an anonymous companion.

The tides erupt and sweep the banks intemperately. Giant goddesses, they retreat and dive back into the ocean of forgetfulness. The sea drowns its never-ending indifference in innumerable blues. Springtime tumbles down on Cordouan as the winter rain had drenched it in mud. It brings balms and perfumes.

The Gestapo's black cars are crisscrossing the streets and avenues. A tide of wrath rises in the occupying force. Through the use of a poster, Von Postel announces that a new attempt on the life of any German will cause twelve hostages to be taken. Jews try fleeing, hiding. All they can do now is to explore the night over footbridges of defacement only to end up on islands where death languishes.

Your mother hides her hair under a gray net. She goes out to the market and meets a strange man who promises her a passage. To you he seems nameless, faceless, with his hat coming down over his nose. He lounges on a bench and reads his paper. Sometimes he throws seeds to the turtledoves and talks to the children in the park. You call him the man in black, for no reason, perhaps because of his sadness or yours. You imagine him in front of a mirror as he takes off his hat and muffler to see his face tense with fear and doubt. His eyes without any light stare, flat and miserable, and you wonder whether he doesn't like your mother. Sometimes he speaks in a rush, a long flow that throws itself into the ocean to end up somewhere else.

The church bells ring the evening angelus. The man pulls his hat down and vanishes into the night. Your mother does not know your father is dead. She can't forget the penetrating looks clinging to her life across their story of happiness, simplicity, and pain. Chance has marked her to the very end with a fragility as transparent as a soap bubble. She falls asleep in her loneliness, she wants to die so she can sleep.

Father, you go out into the night and your fading steps go off with the childhood you lost, your dreams, the war and its madness. Cordouan has been extinguished, a firefly drowning in the sea to hide its light. You follow the coast and forget you are a Jew. The silence and the darkness are frightening but you want to get back to your rock to watch the white stars in the mist.

Suddenly a shadow is outlined. You dream of the gods who rule the waters beneath the starlight. That distant shape resembles a naiad perhaps. The wind flies around her, she dances and places her toes on the sand with water-breaking grace. Between the sky and the sea there is only she, a weightless swirl of sand. She stops, looks around and, thinking she is alone, she dances and throws scattered kisses to the currents and the waves. A pleasure goddess, she slips into the sea and floats in the wave caressing her.

The night is warm, you are watching her and feel the turmoil of the sea inside you, the shiver of a first desire. Thunderbolts draw paths of light in the clouds. You want to touch that dancing shadow. There is almost no distance between sky and earth, just a few rivulets of rain. You run toward her, she is coming out of the sea to your rock, your secret. Then you recognize Aline who, with eyes and dreams in tow, is in the same class as you are. For you the feeling is in the body alone, your heart beats, you run to her and in the rain, in the night, she recognizes you.

Her underwear clings to her breasts and belly, she is cold, smiles at you and raises her lips to you. The rain stops, the clouds barely touch each other. You want her and tear at her clothes, her skin is white as moonlight, you take her, "gently" she whispers to you. You hear her cry as a dream rises to the stars, deep inside her you find the cool of the sea again.

The clouds come apart, the moon is a beacon of happiness.

For the Sabbath observance your mother puts a black veil on her head and goes to the synagogue, which now is the cellar of the man in black. Eyes lowered, she turns around to see if someone is following her. Her course is a walk through shadowy alleyways in which she is the stranger, the hunted one, the fugitive. She moves forward and waits for disaster to strike as if she were prophesying the future. Dressed in black and with a doleful heart in spite of sky, birds, and clouds, she knows she will be suffering for a long time, that it will take a long time for her to die.

You follow her and love her like a very small child. The sea and the stars trace scattered lines of light. God is for you a form of freedom, a coincidence or an encounter you have not yet experienced, but you go with your mother and that roaming man in black.

Despite injustice and defeat, you must move forward on these morning-filled paths. The sun rises, guardian of the world, like the most handsome of gods. For you it retains the face of victory, of eternity.

You raise your eyes toward the light and Aline is dancing for you. Her body has the color of pale sun, delicate glimmering. You no longer hear the sounds of war, you follow your mother, it is mild and warm.

Flames are burning in the bronze candlesticks. They tremble and sway as the men, women, and children repeat their subterranean chant. They are pressed close together in a swoon of perspiration, fear, and hope. An old man in white speaks solemnly. He could expand the light, the sound of his voice has the purity of prayer, the strength of genius. Suddenly he sings and his canticle resonates in sacred music and infinite mercy.

The faces watch the wavering flames, throwing spots on the gray walls. In the clergyman's words they unravel the mysteries and certainties of a distant land beyond the seas, a country of prophets where milk and honey flow. Father, for you the scent of bodies, the shimmering candles, the sad eyes, the imploring hands belong to other people. Their song of prayer rises to the sky like a white soul, then falls back down and is extinguished in a forgotten cellar in Cordouan.

Father, you have not yet encountered God, perhaps

you never will. For me you are the solitary man walking along the sea in a mysterious quest of the infinite and of life. You go to your classes at the teachers' college and try to touch Aline in order to find her again, desire her a little more, and keep her. She is distant … The world's whirlwind is lost in the sea, in the purity of billows.

Von Postel remains a block of ice and silence. The blood of the German, dragged onto the pier, must fall back down on Cordouan, drop by drop. Sentiment and morals are superfluous. The game has rules, each side its duties. Conquerors and conquered have a sense of honor and shame that do not connect.

The Gestapo exposes an intelligence service that works to the advantage of what it calls the enemy powers. The network informs London about troop movements, the presence of ships in the harbor, and about sentries thrown on the beaches after they have been killed by those still confident in life. The oppressing forces hamper freedom but do not yet stifle the spirit.

Father, the mind is the great benevolence of God.

The days go by in shrouded aromas. You follow the outlines of the beach, your eyes lost in the night, in love, in war; you are Aline's captive and her shadow floats beneath the moon. She hardly speaks to you, she has forgotten your breath on her body, your starlit dreams. The sun falls into the sea, rocked by a golden flute.

Your mother is sad and silent. The man in black is there. For you he creates adversity in the mists of silence.

The days vanish in heavens of light but one night, right in the middle of the night, a fire storm comes down on Cordouan. The allied planes discharge their terrifying rain of bombs framed in Bengal lights. They fall farther than the target and destroy a suburban area, an avenue and some houses at the town's entrance. The fire rages, rescuers find only corpses.

Father, you cross through this slaughterhouse of

men and lean against a wall still hot from the flames. Mad with terror, children cry and are looking for their mothers, the wounded howl in pain, dogs are barking, and rats come out of their holes.

The dawn has lost its silences, a page of horror has been engraved in the depths of your memory, a page creased with rage.

It is Easter Sunday. The bell tolls reverently for the burial of the dead, just another wisp of smoke going up in thin air, a requiem for hope. In your garden the mimosas are full of springtime.

Cordouan at night, at war, squelches its houses, its laughter, its dreams. The fountain flows in droplets of gentle music. You cross your town, its scent of ashes trailing, and in order to forget the pain, yours and that of others, you think of Aline, her ivory skin, her face pale with pleasure.

A single light is burning in Cordouan, resembling a ray of moonlight, escaping despite the darkness from the White Tavern in the Rue de la Victoire. There, in a place of warmth and shadows, winners and losers meet without understanding one another. They make fantastically shaped outlines on the walls and ooze a same smell of alcohol, tobacco, and sweating bodies.

The White Tavern is a den edged with mirrors reflecting the wavering flames, the ruby color of wines, the breath of passions. This is where the accidents of love and death connect to dissolve life. A musician plays the piano, another the violin. Each carries his pain, his illusion within, and their music seems to be a story of themselves, disappearing into the night, into oblivion.

Father, you are walking toward the tavern, its light a small bit of happiness, a color melting into the darkness. Some trepidation keeps you outside, a jealous possession of yourself, of what you are hiding and preserving. Then, without thinking, you put your face against the window. Your dreamy gaze glances in. German officers are raising their glasses, girls are treating them to words, pleasures, the magic of caresses. You think of the most beautiful nymphs seized by satyrs. The light pulls a veil of mist over the tables, the guests, and Von Postel. There he is, his monocle seems to conceal his instincts. He looks as if the universe were held in reserve for him and his nobleman's hands are touching Aline.

Close to him, Aline shows him her eyes, her lips, her half-open blouse. You imagine the wandering fingers, the tender looks, and the windowpane is saturated with your breath like an opaque white last page that cannot be read. Your sadness plunges deep into your entrails. For you Aline is the shimmering woman, a sea angel who crumples her underwear to give you a thrust of that body, that heart which you believe to be celestial.

The night lights its stars one by one and slowly burns your heart.

The victorious and all-powerful German army is fighting on three fronts. The eagle unfolds its enormous wings but, worn-out, its wounds are slowly draining its blood. Von Postel offers his condolences to Cordouan's inhabitants in a neutral and anonymous voice. The time of danger topples times of illusion. He blames the civilian population for the dreadful coincidence whereby the enemy air force pulverizes the harbor while the German ships are in dry dock. Soldiers suffer humiliations, snipers increase, and in the countryside attacks swell in number. Generosity and patience have become a luxury. As a man Von Postel understands the resistance and he will ruthlessly oppose it.

Flames turn into ashes. In his hour of solitude, Von Postel listens to solemn and deep-toned music and thinks that the same notes create both life and death.

Suddenly he is afraid and needs a great country so that he can drown his conscience and his success, all mingled with blood and violence. His life opens onto a delusion for, in his weakness, he is his own prisoner. Around him the dusk snuffs out the world and he still stands upright at the edge of the abyss. He dreams, he could have been a motionless fisherman on a blue beach or a reverential passerby in a church where he would kneel and ask for forgiveness. But close to him the embers are losing their gleam and the evening wind falls with the night.

At that same hour your mother lives in obscurity, she blows out her candle and gets into bed in a dark room. In that shadowy, hunched over, frail silhouette disappearing in a space now too large for her you can no longer find the smiling mama of Floirac, your father's lover. You think you see an old woman ready to die.

At the house of the man in black they find a radio transmitter. The roof of his house was blown off by the explosion and in the rubble the German police discovers its sublime Easter gift in the back of a cracked open kitchen. There will be no passage any more.

Dusk falls over Cordouan in a boiling volcano extinguished in the water.

Dawn erases a façade of pink happiness, of pale light, of night. The departure takes place in trucks going to the cattle cars. Jews, resistance workers, passersby, innocent people. Your mother and you. Not one of you looks at the rocks, the sea, a feeling of black soot and fear suffocates every one of you. The heat is oppressive, your eyes meet in overwhelming silence. The minutes flow by slowly and indecipherably. You belong to those ill-fated peoples who walk only to die in a common grave, their eyes wide open in pain and despair.

The officers and soldiers shove the inhabitants of Cordouan with rifle butts. Their glares are cold and aggressive. In the commercial quarter trucks await the victims who have been torn out of their sleep, their dreams, their sky, their habits, their last burst of laughter. Father, forgiveness, too, is a benevolence of God.

The day is a cascade of lights, of dried rivers, and arid heat. The cattle cars have spent the day in the sun and have been turned into ovens. Meant for thirty men, eighty are crammed in. To perish by smothering is one way to die. It is a shorter death, happening with the same indifference as the wind falls or the stars are extinguished. The people imagine the pain in their bodies. Their eyes take on a color of peril and stone.

Father, you try to help your mother, to support her as she mounts the last step into the car. You fear that frailty that is turning her lips and eyes colorless. The man in black emerges, pushed by a sentry. His fate no longer exists for the others, it no longer exists for you. He is not responsible for the disaster, the culture of war alone is enough. Beyond, the sea is magnificent, the currents are no longer shaped by the wind. The water is smooth and firm, the mirror of the sun.

Piled into the cars, going off to a place where people no longer have the strength to stand up. The Germans refuse to leave a single door ajar. To survive you have to stay in a vertical position, motionless and silent. It is a sweating, shouting free-for-all. You understand that the least dangerous position is tightly in a corner of the car where the pressure of the others is less. That is where you put your mother and you form a screen to ward off any knocks against her. She says nothing, the heat has made her beautiful, almost, a physical gentleness pulls you toward her. You have to protect her, she lowers her face, sweat beading on her forehead.

The men have swallowed the last bottles of beer and wine and drink their own sweat to fight off thirst. The latrine buckets are overflowing. People relieve themselves on the floor if they can. Some are throwing up, others shout for something to drink.

Night falls slowly and makes the metal colder. The prisoners collapse in heaps in their own vomit and excrement. Carbon dioxide increases, people breathe it in and die. You are soaking in sweat, in an odor that is human, cruel, and offensive. You are waiting for the night, for then there will be no sun, no rays, the way a burn victim dreams of a freshwater lake.

The smell adds another refinement to the barbarity. The cars roll on. The sea moves away toward an eternal and distant death. The hate machine blindly turns. Not one leader has the courage to disengage the crushing mechanism. In the stations the cars are not opened, water is given once a day, and those who have died by asphyxiation pile up. At noon men shout for something to drink. Father, I shall repeat the word *man*, for in the horror you think you lose what is human in these lifeless faces, filled with fear, but who tomorrow will be real men, the least cowardly, the greatest, the most silent.

People can no longer endure their skin, their sweat, their breathing. They go naked, some feel an erotic desire in a last unhealthy sensuality. Others vomit and die. The corpses are stacked up in the back of the car. Your mother is silent, words remain glued to her suffering, to the abyss.

At the same time, in Cordouan, Aline is walking on the beach. The breeze is soft and moist. She throws rose petals on the waves where they float like tiny white boats. The light shimmers on the breakers.

The train rides on in the sun. You lean against the side of the car. Visions veil your memory — the linden trees in Floirac, the light on the forget-me-nots and the eternal swell, mistress of the world, distant, so distant. Your father lies dying like a human animal in a cellar of the Gestapo and the cattle cars carry people off, desiccated ghosts coming undone from thirst.

The convoy comes to a halt. Will the Germans come to remove the dead? But the cars move again. They haven't even opened the doors. Perhaps at the next station or perhaps at the last one?

The train starts swaying. The exhausted people do not know where they are going. Some proffer obscenities. You think you are going to faint, your mother pulls you up, shakes you, and says very quietly:

"David, you must defy death and pain, you'll end

up by being happy."

They are the only words you hear, the voice is already weak, wasted, far away. You are distracted and think you imagine mystical music that stops the torment. The sea is close to you as if it had not died.

You faint... They throw you on top of the corpses. The train rides on toward infinity. Infinity is far.

You, abandoned on a heap of dead bodies in a smell of urine and sweat, you don't know where your journey ends. The tracks have no itinerary. Obsessed with the men, women, and children who belong to a same family, a same memory, a same future, you wait for another stop, another station.

The train stops. You hear dogs barking and suddenly think that life does exist elsewhere, outside, even for dogs. Officers hurl orders in German. You do not move since you are dead. Finally they remove the corpses. Your heart beats to the breaking point and yet you are dead. But for you, to save you, there are the other men, their shouts, their anger, their revolt. This lack of humanity or its excess is your salvation. The door opens, a breath of wind sweeps through the car, a dry, warm, dust-filled wind.

They remove the dead, and you too, your mother knows it and says nothing. You have to pick the instant in which to flee. Your heart is beating in your temples and your limbs, which are ripping you apart. The breeze cools your death sweat. On the left side the train adjoins the tunnel wall. That is what you must cling to in order to get out of the station. An escape is a question of courage and luck.

The train starts up again. You jump onto the step on the wall side. Shots are wasted or maybe not, the cars leave the tunnel on burned and blackened tracks. The sky is beautiful and hot, the sun is losing its brutality.

Father, you let go of the train on the edge of a ravine and tumble down, curled up, flayed by thorns and gravel. Pulled down the slope without being able to stop, there is grass at the bottom of the ravine. Blood flows across your eyes and face.

The dusk is blue and gray, clouds swell up pink, you hear the rustling of water and it's a return to childhood, the sea, the sun falling into the waves. Night comes in satiny solitude. You fall asleep, the train rolls on, the tracks shredding the earth. The cars are the color of mud and dried blood and cross through lands of thorns where strange animals devour children, women rip their lace garments to show bones where their breasts should be, and exhausted men with faces, in which every feature seems to be a scar, toll the bells. The train penetrates into some underbrush with dead leaves. Its whistle blows and wakes you. The sky is golden and metallic. A shooting star traces a line of light.

Father, you founder in wanderings, silence, and sadness like all the world's fugitives who ask forgiveness for a wrong they have not committed. Each dusk endures in a flickering of fire, it is so beautiful to you, looking for a place between heaven and earth where you can find your life again despite its wounds and distorting mirrors. You walk southward, to the Pyrenees, Spain, toward freedom.

Stars glow and burn out in the greenery of parks. Aline comes back to you and bruises your memory, her pink lips, her mouth raised up to you. How to get her out of your mind without cutting away a piece of yourself, and then the deferred bitterness that is love with a fruitless desire to forget? Touching her body disappearing into the gray foam. The stars are dancing for Aline, the night is dazzling.

You trek across strange cities that outline silhouettes of citadels and at night you sleep in damp hay or under a linden tree with its buttery smells. Your wandering is a certainty of life that stops nowhere, not at the foot of a temple, not at the end of a blind alley. That bit of sea, of rift, of grief fills your mouth again and you are waiting for a man's look to guide and save you.

In a thicket a stranger offers you a cigarette. It is a first and what luxury in war time! The gray curl of smoke rises like a dancing snake. A child is running with his kite that gets caught in a tree. You bring it down for him. He comes near you on the bench and rests his blond head on your lap, golden ringlets like waves of sun. He smiles at you, reassuring you, takes some candy from his pocket and gives it to you. When he leaves, his kite sketches a fleeting line against the sky. A woman chases you away, swearing at you, for you are lingering close to her display of pitiful rotten apples, shriveled oranges, the images of war, hunger, dead flowers.

You walk southward and come to a town that lies sleeping as if dust and despair had retreated into the ridges of the façades, the frailty of sleep, the rooftops of the night. It is dark, so dark, but you are able to decipher the words "Our-Lady-of-Zion" engraved in stone. Eucalyptus trees cover the gate with leaves, shadows, and apparitions. The doorbell is muffled, distant, you wait with pounding heart. Behind the bars, windows, and gardens appears a trompe-l'oeil, which a painter forgot to illuminate.

A nun edges forward with stooped shoulders, her walk belonging to a ritual that resembles her life. She seems like a nocturnal ghost one would not be afraid to touch. Close to the gate, a candle outlines a reflection of worry on her face. You infer each other's image, each other's anxiety, the expectation. You say "Mother, hide me." She answers so softly that you can hardly guess her words: "I have no more room here, my child."

And yet the key turns in the lock and something burns inside you that is neither happiness nor sorrow but hope. The gate creaks, the night is liquid, the nun whispers "Come in, my child."

In the convent of the Ladies-of-Zion the cellars are crammed with Jews. The mattresses on the floor serve as berths, parlors, and refectories.

They had to cross Cambo-les-Bains and then arrive in Spain at Dancharia, the border town. They obtain false papers and one of the Ladies of Zion, Mother Mary of the Passion, simulates the signature of the police commissioner. It is she, the woman at the door lighting a candle in order to show others behind the gate that somewhere a light shines.

A Jesuit father they call Thaddeus guides them

across the Pyrenees. They leave at dawn, four at a time. He has that athletic and healthy bearing that hides a secret, he begs for the freedom of others when some of them see only darkness. He has no words but huge white teeth and a reassuring smile. His skin is dark, lined by the sun, by long marches. As long as the war lasts and oblivion and indifference mask the faces of those who are suffering, he will never have a last journey. The mystery of his life is hope shedding its lights deep into the night, despite wind and rain.

Thaddeus leaves the Ladies of Zion. You follow him together with a woman and two children. The dawn is blue and pure. All men walk toward their destiny with their shattered dream and their despair deep inside them.

To pass from one world into another, crossing hills in the heart of the countryside, terrified, anguish clutching at your throat, your body, your heart. To go from the nocturnal world in which blackouts douse all lights, headlights of cars, lights in windows, and then to see from a hilltop the tiny lights of Spanish villages emerge. To pass from one world into another, a happy past inside you destroyed by the memory of bruised stares, sweat, and above all rage.

A ship raises anchor in Barcelona. You wonder whether it is the shape of an idol the sea absorbs or a mysterious ocean liner frozen on an inert sea. For you and the others, it is the ship sliding on azure, tracing a path of foam in the furrows of the waves toward Judea, Samaria, and Galilee — such an ancient ground which the Jews call the Promised Land, where Christ died to save mankind, and where Islam kneels to pray to Allah. The Land Promised by every promise.

Father, there are the world's springtime seasons, dawns, joys, a warm body you love and forget, life awaiting, larger than the night opening up, than the ocean suppressed. Father, I offer you my hope-filled wishes to start anew, to love again. You have lost Aline's face but there will be evenings of mellow moonlight for you. You will interpret new faces to forget Cordouan, your father, your mother, the flame of candles, the sea's wild dreams, and exhilarations.

A ship awaits you to take you to a distant country, a Promised Land that emerges from the mists of the Orient, mists the gentleness of the sun evaporates.

A cry of joy, a fantastic hurrah erupts from one and all! They run to the railing. The land appears like a fertile goddess, History's muse, arms silvery with foam. The ship's prow breaks the waves into spirals, the sea is drawing arcs and shapes. The faces around you relax. From afar, Jaffa resembles a floating palace with water-moistened shadows, a city that already has a prize, a voice, and hope. On deck the men, women, and children see before them a world as new as a fiancée discovering her future husband in a magic mirror. Palestine lies gleaming in the sun. On the waves the clouds are not really white.

Father, I don't know whether you arrived in Jaffa on one of these phantom ships that flee from the patrols on the Mediterranean or if you had the benefit of a legal crossing without suffering fear and a wish to die.

Your ship resembles all the others since, between heaven and earth, float pink and gray lights, all the world's dreams and destiny's secrets.

There is a photo pasted in your journal, the one of a deck overflowing with people and, attached to the mast like sloppy laundry, an enormous banner in English that reads: "Nothing can keep us from our Jewish homeland."

Is that a picture of the ship you arrived on or did you later photograph those who were arriving to establish a point of departure, yours or that of others? An image is more powerful than a memory. It registers a story in which nothing can be inverted, neither beauty nor ugliness.

You arrive in Jaffa and from the gangway you sense that something larger than your life has been given to you. Loneliness grips your heart with the taste of extinguished charcoal. The harbor has the color of summer's end, of pale sunlight. Palm trees stretch like supple columns.

The ship casts anchor and the currents stop. Life speeds up, new, without innocence, spellbound with escapes, memories, and future. In the falling dust of evening Jaffa gives off an aroma of tenderness.

Father, you go through Jaffa. Children are playing ball in a vacant lot. The railroad runs along the coast with bohemian laziness. The light is magnificent when the sun is low. Rachel opens her doors to you. She offers her race a place to stay and a hospitality that comes straight out of an Oriental dream. There are a dozen of you at her house, Jews from the West waiting for the official reception to take you to the kibbutz.

Rachel seems to be hiding inside a mystery, she is a worn-out woman. Besides doubling her chin, her obesity displaces masses of flesh and air on every side of her. Her booming laugh echoes in her bulk, which is a true sound box. A jolly widow, or simply a widow, her house has many rooms that open onto a huge hallway in which columns seem to protect spaces now too skimpy for her. Born in Jaffa in this middle-class house, then later finding herself there without mother and father, she installs a husband. His only bulk was a thick black mustache, growing heavy when he spoke. Presently, his photograph stands enthroned on the piano in the shade of enormous artificial flowers and stalks of wheat. A glimmering multicolored vase adds to this extravagant palette. Rachel speaks of her early deceased husband only as "my life." Her "life" liked to smoke, loved the music of Bach, and suffered from allergies in summer. He existed merely to provide her with the status of a married woman. Crushed by her just as his photo is by the stalks and flowers, he moved through the hallway, the boudoir, and the bedroom biting on his cigars the way a punished child chews on its fingers. Sometimes he would chomp on his nails out of boredom and he'd rather stroke his mustache than his wife. He had the good taste to depart from this life very quickly and Rachel wept because she had nothing else to mourn.

Now Rachel opens her house to disembarking Jews and tells her life story to all of her boarders. The bedrooms have grown too small for her but not for the others. Only the large drawing room always stays closed, it has two interior windows looking out over the hallway but the panes are colored and opaque and show nothing. You wonder whether it is decked out with paneling, silk fabrics or art objects or if it is empty and abandoned. The charm of Rachel's drawing room is its suppressed silence and nocturnal darkness, a mystery, locked and its key lost.

Rachel's house stands on the great square of Jaffa, close to the seraglio where the British flag flies. Horse-drawn carriages wait for customers. The Palestinian coachmen smoke, chat, and sometimes spit on the ground. They look at the clock that has stopped and wait for the day their country will be liberated from the British Mandate.

The Arabs want a free and independent Palestine. Great Britain continues to be the prison warden of the Orient.

Father, the sky comes down over the motionless blue sea. The blood of your childhood rises up in you. For you, far-off Europe, consumed by the war, stands tall on ruins and tombs. This new land, with its calm and slow wind, is thousands of years old. It creates dreams and visions for every persecuted Jew. It offers them a shore, seasons, a history.

You are now in a street in Jaffa, close to the soap factory and you are engrossed in watching the pyramids of soap blocks that look like trunks of palm trees, towers, lighthouses. Their smell mixed with the laurel leaves is pure and strong. It reminds you of one of your mother's scents, the touch of her skin, a return to childhood. Outside the brightness of the sun is harsh. You blink your eyes due to the powerful light. Suddenly rifle shots ring out. Jewish killers are setting up an ambush for the British high commissioner, Sir Harold Mac Mickael who is suspected of being sympathetic to the Arabs. He is in your field of vision, defeated and pale, and for you has the face of a moment in which blood flows, stops, and coagulates.

Great Britain makes promises to the Jews. Churchill declares to Weizmann: "I have dismembered Palestine, I shall unify it again and dismember it a second time. You can be sure that at the end of the war you will have the largest piece of the cake." Other words were to follow, would not remain unspoken. Time digs furrows, epochs, heavens and hells.

And then, always alone, you lose and find yourself on the piers wet with dampness and mud, on slow-paced avenues. There are too many people around you, the space is large and there are shadows on the walls, the air is wilted. The only reassurance is Rachel's laughter. When you go away from her you still hear it, but it tightens your throat and has a taste of disquiet. Laughter by day, sadness and loneliness at night. Rachel is gentle, fat, vulnerable.

Time is full of holes, you have to wait. Your life stops at uncertain bifurcations. The office of the Jewish Agency of Tel Aviv has to direct you to a kibbutz. You, a blond man playing on his memories, wait and live in Jaffa. Suffering never crosses your lips, but resounds deep inside you in a stifled song. The city and its streets, full of animation and idle passersby, grow familiar. The men sometimes wear red fezzes, others whose wives are bedecked in every color in the world come in from the villages. Their gold dangles in light chains on their forehead or around their neck in coin droplets. Some of them wear gigantic headdresses reminiscent of the fairies in folk tales. In Jaffa's souks, the village adds an imprint of folklore mingled with a wild aroma. Other women who pass by seem to come out of one of those Parisian high fashion houses where styles and wallets are made and destroyed. They are languidly elegant, East and West mixing in flowing and fluid lines.

Shop window follows upon shop window in silhouettes that move — gaudy textiles, multicolored carpets, turquoise or pink eiderdowns, tobacco, spices, sweets, and jewelry. Souks are an escape inventing the image of a city in which life is busy from dawn to nightfall. It is the story of an ageless Orient.

Suddenly your gaze stops at the potter. He is turning his wheel and with his hands shapes the clay that gives its all to him. He watches the forms he is creating the way a mother smiles at the child just born. Finally, with a last caress already tinged with forgetfulness, he places them on shelves.

In the back of the shop, a half-light shines more brightly than an autumn glow. There, around a table, four adolescent girls are painting colored flowers on vases and jars. Then in blue or white they write Jaffa on them. They don't talk and seem to be posing for a live photograph. Their faces are without make-up, without pain. You fuse them in a mirror where adolescence is pure and bland. Suddenly the oldest of them raises her eyes and pushes back her dark hair filled with a scent of lavender grass. Her large black eyes shine slightly then look back down at her work. You watch her, she barely blushes and no longer stirs. You feel like touching her but move on.

In a vertigo of bewitching sounds, the crowd in the souk brings luxury, effusion, and dust to a foreign city.

In the mingled silences of the tepid summer nights, the muezzin's voice is rousing. It drifts in deep-throated grooves from one minaret to the next and repeats a mysterious sounding prayer you don't understand. The muezzins chant in the pink light of dawn. Bells of churches and convents ring in the new day. In prayers, God is the One God in the land of prophets.

Father, you rise from your bed, the house is dark and empty. The street noises offer a remote premonition of life. Coolness ascends from the depths of the earth and rain is falling in threads of silver. Silence puts the house to sleep, then stops. All of a sudden steps approach, muffled, heavy, and irregular, and Rachel appears buoyant in some strange reddish apparel. She resembles a carnival ghost, colored by the dreams of other people, in search of a friend, an accomplice, a soul mate. She recognizes you and her laugh pierces the walls and the air. The costume ball at the house of her friend Selim al-Abiad is a success.

Rachel's turban is embellished with artificial stones. Her fuchsia sari exposes a fat shoulder and forearm hugged and pinched with a snake-shaped bracelet. She sways, reels like a fire no longer stoked. Under her Jaipur veils she looks exhausted, drunk, and done in. Her lips are mumbling incoherent words. You put Rachel into the brass bed that is too small for her and she falls asleep. You cover her with a linen sheet hiding her life, her disguise, and her dream.

Day trembles like a pink fog over Jaffa, a danger takes shape inside you in anxious foreboding. The sound of the doorbell, long, loud, and persistent, rips through the house as in Cordouan. You hesitate and see Rachel's things around you like lost pacts, joys belonging elsewhere. You open the door, the British police are there, cold and aloof. The officer is as haughty and arrogant as the empire, teetering nevertheless. A disdainful and vindictive glow makes him look colorless.

Through the window, vehicles, jeeps, and police wagons surrounded by soldiers are parking. You have to make an effort to hear these human voices or even to look straight at the indistinct group already swallowing you up. Your breathing comes with difficulty, your lips are quivering. You were illegal immigrants in Rachel's house. The closing net represents a victory for the English.

They force the bedroom doors, the boarders file out in striped, plain, or unsightly pajamas. The police check papers and make arrests, while the sadistic officer's laugh curdles the blood.

Events come back in blurred and agonizing images. You remember the pallid faces of the boarders in Rachel's house. This arrest surges up in you, a photographic enlargement in which the English are monstrously huge but their faces blurry. You prefer for hate to be badly delineated in your memory and you want it hazy and hidden.

Rachel sleeps and snores. People are thrown into trucks and police wagons with their headlights on. The convoy drives on for a long time, a murky light drowns the horizon, fog trembles over the sea. The whirring of the motors awakens the sleeping city. You are on the way to the British refugee camp in Athlit where illegal immigrants are detained.

Father, you are thirsty again and remember the train that took you away from Cordouan. You are accustomed to fear the way a child goes into a dark room where he stretches out his hand to touch a black background closing in. Jaffa vanishes in the wetness of its first rain, barely moistened, already distant, absent, and swept away by oblivion.

While the trucks move on into the distance, the clandestine radio station Kol Israel, the voice of Israel, that has been silent since 1940, starts its broadcasts up again emitting its calls to the resistance. The convoy moves on. After the rain, the sun, pale and without rays of light, is shining. You look back, the land retreats, throwing back an image of birds flying off.

The camp of Athlit stands by itself in the middle of nowhere, in a desolation of jagged edges. A grim and arid landscape with foreign voices shouting beneath the stars. Lost jackals and wolves are looking for prey, for victims.

The wind blows on Athlit, coming from the sea or some distant desert, but sweeps the same gray walls, gardens without leaves or flowers. All the world's barbed wire looks the same, sandbags heavy with sand, rusty barrels that are never painted and the oppressive, closed air in which time never moves.

The convoy stops. They shove you inside and the British officer screams orders that twist his mouth and face. Father, you arrive in Athlit and already think you are violating the truth of others, those who live behind a fence, even if each one of them hides the nakedness of his life in a secret, in silence. The men before you have a sad look, dark circles under their eyes from insomnia, and the stink of badly washed animals. Hallways seem like labyrinths in science fiction, cracked, slippery, without any exit. The only bright spot in the cells is a ray of sun or a moonbeam through the bars that are too close together, too black while you imagine them painted in white, red or green. Colors are born only from the light.

Then evening falls. The night has a moonlit patina. Mattresses have been thrown down on the floor, there are brown blankets printed with dirty flowers and there is that nauseating smell that sticks to your nose, lungs, and still exists. In the deep of the night, wolves and jackals howl in the silence.

Life in Athlit is snatched from the dawn in the slowness of incarceration. Father, we don't relive our past, we are never the same, but identical days are draining and destructive. Worn-out conversations drown their depth, their mystery, they no longer have any history or memory. The detained lose their nerve because of a rat running between their legs or a cockroach marching across a wall as black as he.

One of those imprisoned in Athlit sings for a woman he loves. She comes from a world only he knows and she has the face he yearns for. She is present and vanishes at the same time, but in the evening when he blows his candle out and lives his daydream he sings to her in his cell. They call him Moses, he is of the age when what matters is love, love's beauty, love's agony. Sometimes the prisoners shout to make him stop, perhaps he weeps in silence then. You can never see anything through the partitions, you can only guess at the wreckage of others.

Thus, Father, you observe the people around you for the first time. Is that so you won't stay insular? On the ship and at Rachel's you seem to move through a space that is theirs without touching them. For you the endless road each person clears belongs to his own trenches of pain, passion, and uncertainty. In Athlit, you stare at others the way a convalescent walks on new soil where the world's dreams get lost. In Athlit there are Jewish immigrants, Palestinian revolutionaries, men of the Church, ulamas of Islam who watch each other and wonder who will be the first to disintegrate. Within himself each one of them churns a shattered dream, a foiled outrage, locked inside the shadow.

There is a photograph of you in Athlit. You are sitting cross-legged on the ground and behind you, seated in chairs, the "important" men of the camp are posing: an orthodox priest, Father Boulos, his hair pulled back in a bun and with an enormous beard that hides his sin of gluttony. A man in white, Michel Mitri, president of the labor union of Jaffa, the Catholic Boutros Asfour, a brilliant business man and activist for independence, a man in a turban whom they call Cheiky, "my sheik," and lastly one of Islam's great ulama, Sheik Ahmed al-Tahi. Only he seems to stand out in the photograph.

Father, are you with them in this picture because they wanted to freeze the faiths of Yahweh, God, and Allah in one single black and white image? In order not to burn one life after another, the indignity of prison was necessary in the name of all freedoms. This Athlit photograph could be the title of a book. It is strange. You are looking into the camera with a sense of anxiety as if before you a huge fire were burning and the flames were approaching you in a smell of cinders.

Sheik Ahmed al-Tahi has the grand appearance of the men of Islam, which they augment with a turban and by floating inside flowing robes that add the full-ness of excessive fabric to their lanky frame. His look is piercing and his slender hands frame his words with a faith in gestures, details, and shapes. Mysterious, his very black eyes hide a light deep inside that comes on and goes off like a will-o'-the-wisp. He has no rival in Athlit. For you there is no one like him. He has studied in London and Paris. He is courteous, subtle, and committed, he speaks to you with obvious compassion, with the clear wish to get to know you.

"My son, do you come from the East or the West?"

"I come from France and I'm looking for a country."

"Everyone's country lies hidden inside him. We give ourselves to the earth and it feeds you, we look at the stars and then they light your way."

"But I have come to the Promised Land."

"My son, who made you that promise? We live by the mercy of God."

His voice is slow, deep, and does not resonate.

"I'm looking for a refuge. I have been hurt."

"Have you ever tortured a man?"

"No."

"Do you look at the moon at night?"

In Athlit nights are cold. Father, you go to your cell and think in spite of yourself that nothing is impossible, for in someone else's voice a here and now exists... Days pass, the autumn progresses in a desire to grow old, to slowly die. Clouds drift and, pushed on by wind and time, they trace magical drawings.

Time moves slowly in Athlit. It penetrates inside without language or silence. It is savage, tragic, invisible, and begs for the future. It slides into nothing. Time stops in prison, but elsewhere in the world life pulses with its hatreds and realities in unspeakable fear. Events go on and on to be catalogued in over-burdened memories where war is a ritual that never ends. Men wear different uniforms to suffer and die. Nights are aflame over Europe and stars collide with the roofs of Athlit.

Sheik Ahmed al-Tahi comes back into the gray room every evening. His face pursues a vision, an image, and his eyes sparkle, sunken with wariness. Deep within him, he holds on to the soul, the hymen of his land, and speaks the way light erupts through the clouds. In a solemn, stable voice, recorded in a written piece of music, he repeats the history of his Palestine, called Israel by some. The country gathers people and religions with their incense and their hymns under the same light. The sun burns the coast cooled by the waves, the olive trees hold on to their leaves in spite of the seasons. And yet, there is a deceptive calm, a false prosperity due to inflation, the war of others, and the feeling of unreality and torment. Peace seems to reign and a wind of reconciliation breathes over yesterday's enemies. The Jews commit to a truce.

Shadows grow larger on the walls of Athlit. Candles quiver and burn in the night. Sheik al-Tahi speaks of what he loves and travels all the way to the end of his dream, beyond fences and bars. His face relaxes, he sees the countryside again where shepherds move through ancient landscapes. There, the wind sings with the cicadas, the melody of flutes tells of the moist freshness of dawn and dusk. The herds listen to the plaintive refrains of these eternal regions and graze the dry grass of the same paths. The Palestinian farmers pick their fruit, extend the same hand, the same gaze to the trees that bring shade and contentment. Orange trees exhale their fragrance and, coming from the beginning of time, the light imposes a motionless and serene tranquillity. The countryside, too, takes its incense and its hymns in tow. But the rustling of the air and leaves barely covers up the terrorism that slowly sets its traps, its brutality, and its sorrows.

Sheik al-Tahi watches the glittering of the stars. His eyes overflow with sadness. He deeply inhales the smell of the land that he wrenches from his prison, his chest, the cold breath of the night. He is older than his birth. Some nights he howls with rage, for the country is infested with subterranean organisms, secret organizations that want to break the truce and cause the English policy to fail. The Haganah becomes the embryo of a national army. A clandestine group of young fighters establishes the Irgun Zvaï Leumi. The Irgun is entirely offensive. The third group, known as the Stern, openly refuses the truce.

Sheik al-Tahi's voice is sometimes tainted and stifled. His gaze grows dense and thick with smoke. In Palestine, his land, a relentless, blistering war is being contained before exploding. Dreadful evidence portents bursts of fire, clouds of dust, and dark blood. Judaization is making great strides but, for him, for the Palestinians, there is no foreign land. If they are called before the tribunal of their history, their childhood, their present, the land belongs to them and their cause is just. They are not really organizing. On the other side, in the opposing camp a spirit of daring prevails.

Father, this is how you learn that every gesture of violence or of compassion belongs to a same cry of Yahweh, God or Allah, but you feel submerged in a world you don't want to lose again. Athlit becomes a fertile ground linking and amassing prisoners, companions of the world's vertigo beyond a photograph and a waiting period. In the deep of the night in the rain's lianas, all of you hear the sound of fine droplets falling.

In Athlit the winter is humid, desolate, and the days are short and slow. Sheik Ahmed al-Tahi has days of great silence. He meditates with his head buried in his hands and stirs only to kneel down at times of prayer. He could almost be drafting a book he isn't writing or scrutinizing a closed world of inviolable depth that is his alone. Sometimes he looks at his hands or perhaps at the blue veins across them and seems to stumble on a feeling of helplessness, of arrested, futile gestures.

On other days, the skin of his face is clear and his look ambivalent but lively. He says to you:

"My son, I'm going to teach you Arabic and Hebrew."

"Two languages at once, that's hard."

"Listen and you'll learn two languages that are both Semitic and have similar phonetics."

He smiles and goes on:

"Salaam, Shalom: peace. Tel Aviv, Tel Rabii: the hill of springtime. At your age, memory is a mirror and it shouldn't become a frozen lake."

Suddenly there is the nauseating smell of the main noontime meal. Crushed wheat again, in a strange mush, and once a week a spoiled orange.

"My son, today I shall not eat at all."

"Neither will I, too bad if I'm hungry during the night."

"Listen, my son. Do you know that anti-Semitism as it is known in the West is an attitude foreign to the East? For centuries, the Jews in Muslim territory have held very specific positions even if nationalist leaders sometimes clashed. On the level of the different social classes there has been assimilation. A cultural exchange took place and, between the two wars, a sometimes harmonious stability existed between our two communities."

"My Sheik, the Jews have suffered continually and everywhere. My father died under torture in a Gestapo cellar and my mother keeps on slowly dying in a camp."

"Injustice is expressed through violence. The world has persecuted the Jews, and you persecute us. Deep beneath the earth, terrorism is incubating like burning magma that will erupt in a volcanic fire."

"My Sheik, can violence be stopped?"

"Through prayer, but people no longer know how to pray."

"The Jews pray for a return to their Promised Land. We are the chosen people and this is our land."

"This is the land of the olive tree, the branch of peace."

Asian nights seem the oldest nights in the world. They touch the reverse side of men and possess their dreams. They are long and the winter hides their stars and moon.

Sheik al-Tahi fasts from dawn to sunset.

"My Sheik, why do you fast?"

"Man lives on the word of God."

"But it isn't Ramadan!"

"The world needs redemption and prayer. In a dream, I saw my people die, drowning in mud, blood, and fire."

"It was a dream."

"Tomorrow the battle will begin. The Arabs are advancing, brave and enthusiastic and carefree because Allah will help them. Facing them are not Semites like themselves any more, but Westerners presenting themselves as a sect with an ancestral philosophy. Rationalism has replaced religion and nationalism is replaced by a culture of science. The Arabs think that the concept alone counts, their cause is just and can only prevail. It is not they who created Dachau and they did not create Auschwitz. Allah will help them. David, my son, we will pay. For the injustice of the West toward you we will pay with our land, with our dead youth, with our disemboweled women and our blinded children. We shall suffer until the dream has been forgotten."

"My Sheik, my father, but the Jews, too, need a land, they cannot wander forever."

"The tribes of Israel were unified in this land throughout their history, seventy years only. Seventy years during thousands of years of wandering. That is the will of God."

The night resembles the apocalypse, a mercy of world's end. Strokes of lightning and torrents of black rain submerge Athlit in a mysterious nightmare where shapes, bodies, and hopes become entangled.

Sheik al-Tahi lights his candle. He consults a book by Abdelkader al Jazeiri, the Algerian Emir who fought the French. He opens it and reads:

"Sometimes you see me as a Muslim, a perfectly sober and pious Muslim, humble and always praying.

"Then you see me running to the churches, tightening a belt around my waist. And I speak in the name of the Son, then in the name of the Father and the

Holy Spirit. The Holy Spirit, that is the outcome of a quest and not of a deception!"

"And then you see me teaching in Jewish schools. I proclaim the Torah and show them the righteous path."

"See, I believe in all that God has sent down regarding Books[*]."

The flame quivers. Mankind is exhausted from the storm's frenzy.

Sheik al-Tahi blows out his candle. The night is a downpour of ink.

[*]*Abdelkader* by Bruno Etienne, Hachette, 1994.

In Athlit there are no white flowers in the spring. The seasons have no ritual, no fragrance, they are cold, luke-warm, or scorching. One morning, a mauve and bluish light awakens the camp. The British officer smiles for the first time. In an English he intends to be superior, peremptory, and contemptuous, he announces the end of the war to the prisoners.

Father, peace has finally come to the world and people once again want the world. Church bells peal the end of the war from one shore to another, from one sky to another. Lost countries, found again but still bat-tered and bruised, come back to themselves. The war has destroyed the idols of conquerors and conquered. People hold on to the pain of suffering, of expunging their sullied dreams. But their faces suddenly have a joyful color, their eyes mysterious, the present erases.

They hope to hear words of life again. The war is over. Springtime mornings rise over Europe. Palestine, though, lies in the shade of olive and palm trees, all along its shores. The light drifts over the water but you would think that it is sinking into a sea of flames.

In Athlit, the Jews, Christians, and Muslims all tell the same stories. There is no humiliation, no conquered people, but there is the horror of the thousands of surviving Jews who have come out of the death camps. Battered, emaciated, their eyes filled with pain, they hope to find refuge in the Promised Land they call Israel. There are more than a million of them coming from all directions, living in a same expectation, that of a homeland where they can finally put down their sandaled feet, stop their wandering, their suffering. What horrors have come away from the camp. Truths are sometimes more outrageous than legends. In Athlit, the prisoners are in torment, there is one land, unique, holy, open with fissures and dreams.

In the distance, the sea presents a dark background beneath a gold-fringed sky. The Haganah, the Irgun, and the Stern— the three Jewish resistance groups — come together in order to make a world they imagine but have not yet understood. They decide to break the truce. A secret pact binds a holy land to the angel of fury. A night of fever, coming from the past of some, drafts the future of others. The water of the fountains flows like a melody sung for idols.

In Athlit, Father Boulos has a visitor and goes back into his cell where his life disappears. Returned from an outside and foreign world, with things turned upside down and emotions blurred, he walks like a monarch who takes the secret of a fraud away with him. He and his shadow form a procession of slow and weighty silhouettes. His eyes have a bitter hint of honey but sometimes a moist reflection softens his face. Father Boulos is obese. Bereft of muscles and energy, he hides a child's heart within. In the evening he returns, balancing his thick and cumbersome anatomy. He speaks. The words part his lips like a wound. His village has been mined and destroyed but in the other villages life continues. Pamphlets have been distributed in public squares, near the fountains and evening fires. Around the braziers when the zithers are played, men tell their families what the Jews are declaring in these papers they read, which the wind propels and blows away. Begin, the leader of the Irgun, informs the farmers and shepherds that he does not wish to cause them any harm. He only alerts them to the fact that the British want to set them up against the Jews. He hopes they will not fall in the trap. The wheel of fate is turning. The Palestinians who despise the British continue to be attentive spectators. Their land has been mined, cleared of mines, and cultivated. Everywhere a red color of exposed rocks remains.

In Athlit, life still seems sterile and snuffed out. Father, you need to go back inside yourself to find a dream again, an escape and a bit of sunshine. Then you suddenly think of a woman's face, the mystery of a single moment in a world dismissed. She slips into you in the absence, her image is hazy, distant. All you love of her is the one look at the potter's place in Jaffa. Does she need a man to take her or is her life already apportioned elsewhere? You see her enormous eyes again, lowered to hide desire and tenderness. Your loneliness is a habit, a test in which the days all look alike. Father, for you and for me love is a road of stars.

Time devours shade and light. Father, the words you write belong to every vanished voice that tells the world its own story wherein life and death come upon each other without being defined. There is no date, so that compassion can come to those who are growing old. You list the events heard on the radio. In Athlit, newspapers come late, they distort the unexpected and slow it down. There are badly printed photos in which you can only guess at the field of ruins of the station of Lydda, the charred stones of the police station of Gibath Olga. Dynamited bridges pile up in exploded mounds, in railroad stations interiors crumble, and the planes of Ksar Kisrin are destroyed.

The days press on. They emerge in silhouettes of fire, inferno, burnt light. A tide of lava consumes images, fields, shepherds, and herds. Lost men, beloved women, and transformed children vanish in blood-smudged crowds. The radio station of the Haganah, Kol Israel, proclaims: "Down with the British Nazi regime oppressing our country."

Father, for whom is this country? This landscape spreads smoke over lilac aromas, expands to deposit its offerings — a rugged hand holds manna from heaven in the desert, in crucified hands there is bread and wine, and in an Islamic temple there is a road of hope. Father, today this land is for you and for me.

In the evening in the countryside, shepherds wander with their herds in the ember-colored dusk. From deep underneath the earth they hear sad voices fading away.

Evening falls. Elsewhere the summer is leaving in a fragrance of faded jasmine and brooks are relinquishing their water. In Athlit, the seasons stop at the end of a plowed road and a building of arid stone. Sheik al-Tahi is lying on his mattress, deathly pale with his hands folded on his chest, his arms already white. His beauty is that of a man contemplating God, coming into His sight. His profile draws a shadow in the light.

"My Sheik, teach me how to live my life. Don't leave me."

"My son, I have taught you Arabic and Hebrew. Life itself will tell you about its woes. I am happy to die, to close my eyes and die. Allah is merciful."

"My Sheik, the land is on fire and drowning in blood."

"I know, my son. For them, victory is killing one

group of people in order to save the other. Do you know why King David did not build the temple of Jerusalem?"

"No."

"Because from the depth of his conscience he heard a voice telling him: 'Do not build a house in My Name, for you have been a man of war and you have spilled blood'."

His words are growing faint, distant, and he is short of breath.

"My Sheik, don't tire yourself."

"Let me pray and die, my child."

The dawn is magnificent. A mellow peace reaches heaven. The sun's rays are climbing up to Allah. Sheik al-Tahi does not wake up. A scent of myrrh floods his cell.

A graveyard silence puts Athlit to sleep. The sentries, like pillars of stone, become one with the place. The night wanders around in mystery, and then a light of the world's end slowly twists into imperceptible and scattered sounds. Clouds hide a full moon.

Armed men are advancing on Athlit. They are invisible and follow the directives their memory has been repeating for days: a map of the place, access to cells, sentry posts, directions to be followed, password... The operation is to take thirteen minutes.

The attack is launched in black silence. Gliding silhouettes, men emerge everywhere. They belong to very small Jewish resistance groups. The raid is so brazen that they have to either believe in it or die. They must liberate the illegal immigrants detained in Athlit. Perfidious Albion will understand that the

Zionists are fighting and that the God of Israel is on their side.

Unfamiliar faces are pulling the prisoners out of their sleep: they must follow, obey without a thought, and leave by an underground passage. Not waste a fraction of time, every minute squanders a thousand seconds. These men, who have come from somewhere else to save their brothers, must command a place they are entering for the first time, a place they touch with a fear of being burned. Grasp and flee, for nothing belongs to chance, everything is wrenched away from life, from death, another time, give or take.

Shots ring out. Athlit is illuminated as if it is bright daylight. Cries escape from deep inside the building, men's voices, voices of all those who are waiting and being abandoned. A smell of gunpowder, flames, and ashes trails behind and is crushed. Then the rumble of a storm comes down on Athlit.

In the distance at dawn, Arab farmers are awakened by a furor coming from an outside world. A child screams that it is the sound of a dragon. His mother covers him up and rocks him back to sleep.

Dawn slips in the birth of torment: large equipment whips the soil, bulldozers churn up stones, huge machines smash boulders. The soft and secret soil becomes disembodied. A fence of barbed wire springs up. It breaks the outline of the dunes, the contour's features. A water tower rises like a missile. With laborious movements, workers set up gray or brown barracks. Worried, the farmers watch. The children's eyes grow wide, they are curious. In the evening, they can all see it clearly. There is a new kibbutz on their land, farther than Athlit, very close to the sea.

At night they share the world. On the one side with

electricity, on the other with candles. In the Arab village, the mother rocks her child to a melody that comes forth from all the world's tender love and innocence:

> *Sleep, my sweet little one, sleep,*
> *I will give you doves;*
> *Don't be afraid of anything, white doves,*
> *I only sing so that my child will sleep.*

Night arranges its beams of stars and sparkles, the moon is oval-shaped.

Trucks are escaping from Athlit, the camp and its prisons can be seen lit up in pyrotechnics. Panic-stricken cries, broken voices vanish in the distance like phantoms in the night. Shots grow sparser and disappear. The trucks forge ahead and move away.

The danger is past. In a delirium of exhilaration and friendship people throw themselves into each other's arms. It could be happiness. The trucks drive on, slow down, move on again. The escapees look at each other as if for the first time. The enthusiasm has been contained, they sit down and watch the trees, the night, pass by. Then, slowly, they discover a new moderation inside themselves. Exhilaration has dropped, muffled and heavy. It is exhausting, it is freedom. They have to invent a dream, a face for themselves.

The trucks stop at the end of a road where a gate in

the barbed wire is opened. There is a water tower, there are brown barracks. It is the kibbutz that will receive the former prisoners of Athlit.

Father, you see your new home before you. It is a gift but it smothers you. Our prisons lie hidden inside ourselves, they are a land from which we can never escape.

A heavyset woman comes over to you, her hair loose and a dynamic look in her eyes. She smiles, her teeth are large and white. She may be huge and maternal, but her voice seems to belong to one of those women of war who repeat the same words. She is talking about the kibbutz and says:

"The land and means of production are the shared property of those who work here, under the direction of each one in turn. Salaries are abolished. The principle, each according to his abilities for each according to his needs, is simple and frees everyone from all worries. Children are raised in 'small republics' and see their parents at recreation time. The system is having astonishing results. It has allowed deserts to be transformed into fertile land by the labor of pioneering Jews. Welcome to all of you."

Father, a path opens before you, covered with yellow leaves fallen in an early autumn. A more cruel path opens in your imagination, made of dry leaves the color of blood. You remember Sheik al-Tahi, who would pray and who taught you Hebrew and Arabic. He should have stayed on, just a little longer, to kiss the ground and caress the earth with you. But a dark vision of black and gray photos reminds you of your tortured father, your mother in the train, Aline giving her body to others, and all the dead faces of the camps' survivors. That is the wound inside you, greater than forgiveness. You can no longer accommodate it, it digs into you, holds too tightly, burns. So much unfulfilled love has turned to hate, to despair that you must give up and scatter. There are sorrows that oblivion does not salvage. You decide to become a member of Irgun.

Father, why do we resemble one another without ever having met?

Because you and I have suffered a great deal before making our choice. We have loved violence so that we could exist.

The sun is a dazzling whiteness. The air is dry but beads of sweat appear on faces, muscular torsos, and shining skins. The training has been going on since dawn. The exhausted men work relentlessly. They each see their own fatigue and freedom in the other ones' eyes.

Father, you are neither taller nor smaller than the rest, you resemble each other like pieces on a Persian checkerboard. You play black and white to win or die. Indoctrinated, trained in commando warfare, you all have a new homeland, a nurturing mother, the Irgun.

Jewish extremism is now expressed. It needs a blotter to dry its stains. A clandestine group of young fighters established the Irgun. In locations that hold a mystery and on bare walls hangs the same map: Palestine, including the two banks of the Jordan River, is crushed by a closed fist over a rifle with the slogan *Rah Kah*, "Only like this."

Why like this? The Irgun is on the offensive. It draws triumph from its action as if, amid the grenades, the light were dancing and dissolving. The members are recruited from every background but especially from among immigrants from Poland. They are the strongest, the most damaged. They have suffered twice, once from being Jewish, the other from being Polish. Their eyes see life as prey. The Irgun has its own radio station, publishes *Liberty*, a newspaper in Hebrew, and *Zion in Combat*, a pamphlet in English and French.

Father, you stride along the narrow, dark hallways and on a brighter wall you think you see a shadow. It is the shadow of the child in Cordouan running along the beach beneath a streak of night and the sea around him trembles like perfumed chiffon. Perhaps you are forgetting who you are. The places around you have soundless walls. You wonder if there isn't a mirror anywhere so you could see your face.

Returning to Jaffa under a white sky so as not to refuse anything to a city that keeps its secret like unfinished literature. Seeing Rachel again in the guise of a bejeweled goddess whose corpulence provides a sad image of fertility, even if her laughter brings her close and palpable. Following the vanishing road one bright morning and then discovering a solitary river on the way to Jaffa, the al-Auja, flowing close to a water mill. Touching the intact things that look at time without a shudder.

Father, you sit down under a palm tree, the water is clear, the mill turns like an ancient clock. The breeze is soft. Suddenly, laughter rings out like shriveled leaves flying off. In their Sunday dresses some young girls approach who have just picked oranges they put in a basket covered with a white cloth. One of them says she wants to go to Bethlehem for Christmas, the other answers that she is more interested in love than in prayer. A third one sits down as if she weren't listening to the others or as if she belonged only to herself. She opens her flared, flowered dress, her breasts are full, her waist is slender. She has lilacs in her hair.

In that white and blue light a strange joy is born within you, Father. You hesitate, move forward, and recognize the girl from the Jaffa pottery, her quiet look that comes out of a tale in which only poetic fairies exist.

The earth turns like a crystal roof. Then you hear her sing. Her words seem like soap bubbles flying off.

> *Do not kiss me on my eyes*
> *That would be a farewell kiss.*
> *Kiss me on my lips,*
> *For our words are everlasting.*

The song has ended. You go over to her and hear yourself speaking Arabic.

"Where am I actually?"

She laughs, her eyes are perceptive, she says:

"In Palestine."

She looks at you curiously.

"You're Jewish and you speak Arabic?"

"A little."

She rearranges the lilacs in her hair, pushes a rebellious lock aside and asks: "And where are you going?"

You smile and answer:

"To Palestine."

She offers you an orange, you take it, and look at her eyes which have lost their silence. You say:

"That is the most beautiful orange in Palestine."

Rachel gives you tea and cookies from England. Her parlor is closed with even more dust. She talks of useless and worldly things and laments the victims of the attacks. Her chatter wears you out but how can you possibly tell her you are a member of the Irgun.

In her presence, at her house, you barely hear her and in your mind's eye you see instead a sequence that belongs to your previous night. Are you really its per-petrator or a strange character haunted by a dream he is trying to forget? You are walking beneath the light of stars at night. A silent freedom imposes a semblance of life on the landscape in a nocturnal world. A quiet sound moves through the foliage and in the motionless shade you see a gazelle feeding its little one. You take your weapon and fire, there is blood. The gazelle's sad eyes stare at you as she dies.

Rachel talks. She offers you more tea. The cookies are delicious you tell her, but then she excuses herself. She has a card game at her friend Majida's, whom she loves, an exceptional woman who has fired her maid and passed her on to Rachel.

She kisses you. You leave her and walk along the sea. That is where you were born, at the end of a world that is drowning. The waves roll in the wind, in the deep abyss of the water. Again you see the sorrowful eyes of the gazelle and her child, they take on the color of a bruised sea. The swell distorts your face, your gaze, your dream.

Jerusalem is the color of a flameless fire. The dusk illuminates it with a copper, honey-colored mist. The city stifles its last clamor before night falls when it withdraws into itself, into its silence.

Father, sitting on a rock, your eyes wide open, you see it for the first time from the heights of the Mount. In an intense chill, the olive tree carries a fragrant trail of aged leaves, of a trunk a thousand years old, of faded bark. Jerusalem protects its enclosure, its Wailing Wall, its church bells, and its minarets. And you love it with grave anxiety as if its incomparable beauty might turn cruel. The city, so unreal for you until this moment, seems to you sublime, bitter, and onerous. Yet, the breeze disperses an Oriental languor, a breath that spawns the world's creation. The dusk is gone and Jerusalem reveals a luminous soul descending from the intention of God.

The night watches. The city, grown old from so many promises, offers its peace, its wounds, its history. Beneath this same, always blue sky, Solomon wanted to build a temple, Jesus knelt down to suffer and die, and Mohammed wanted to ascend to heaven. Jerusalem presents a boundlessness in which the real world, man's spirituality, begins. Father, you are an exile and already denying the city at your feet. Your loneliness assails you, it is no longer a renunciation but creates itself and changes to commitment. Tomorrow, you will attack the central prison of Jerusalem.

The night is long. Dawn moves in, strange and pink. Father, you have become a terrorist, it is crazy how alike we are! Tomorrow two people will be dead. A torrential rain cleanses the corpses on the sidewalk. The face of violence has become familiar to you, reassuring. Your hands are bare but no longer white. You hide your eyes and weep. It will be the last time.

Far away, in Cordouan, lightning crashes down on the sea.

Father, you go toward the beach. A glow lies buried in the rocks, the sand. A moist smell and the quivering of the water expose your emotions, your desire. For you the sea is a perpetual pathway toward childhood, entombed tenderness, expired purity. For you, the world flees into its deserts, its secrets, but it endures. Hope endures and, in the distance, ships arrive borne by the waves and iridescent foam. They moor on the shores and shimmer in the night. They then resemble temples of light. These ships coming from everywhere bring people to the land, survivors of the Nazi camps, former Palestinian exiles, and Jamal al-Husseini who is coming to reawaken the Arab resistance. Heaven watches over and protects every dream.

Father, you watch the different people arrive. Jamal al-Husseini stores up the bitterness of exile. His sensitivity and his intelligence sharpen a desire for battle and victory. The inertia in which his brothers have sunk exasperates and annoys him. He states that Ibn Saud of Arabia and Farouk of Egypt have declared their support for the Palestinian cause. The Jews, too, come pouring into a land where orange trees sag beneath their fruit, grain ripens beneath the rays of gold, and soap spreads a scent of faded laurel leaves.

Jamal al-Husseini returns to the country and believes he will overwhelm the world. With an automatic gesture he takes off his fez and strokes it, hiding his thoughts. In a last movement without violence, he touches his mustache and proclaims a general strike everywhere in his land of Palestine.

Stopping in its tracks, the world will stir.

Sundays pass and, between two escapes, others come and place themselves at the center of man.

Close to the orthodox diocese of Jaffa, you linger after some tea at Rachel's house. The wintry sun plays with its pale shadows. The bishop leaves the church, preceded by his attendant tapping his cane on the ground to announce the venerable man who follows him. You observe his costume, embroidered in gold and pearls. He moves along, impervious, untouchable, and cries out when his cane does not sufficiently frighten the passersby.

Suddenly a white group drifts by. A procession of fabulous creatures emerges from the church. Young girls surround a bridal couple and throw flower petals at them under a winter sun. The light is a subdued blue. A dwindling song comes from inside, a Byzantine hymn reverberates, spiraling in incense and perfumes.

"In glory and dignity, oh God, may you marry them."

The bride and her bridesmaids wear the same crown of flowers in their hair, covering their faces. They are a vision of white and satin. Tulle and jasmine draw garlands.

The guests come out of the church. They throw rice on the bride. A huge, heavyset woman ululates. Father, you can hardly contain your laughter, a nightingale's voice emerging from that elephantine shape. You think of those fairy tales in which the couple is married and with many children lives happily ever after, but your life lies elsewhere. You are on an island where death whistles and stops. At night your stomach hurts. You are hostage of yourself and of your mutilations.

The young girls encircle the bride. One of them scatters petals over you. You are taken aback, her eyes expect you, she smiles and says:

"Shalom."

It is the girl from the pottery shop in Jaffa. A strange light blurs her outline, her tulle, her pallor. Light from within makes her glow, already setting her aflame. You hold your breath, yet it is you who say:

"You are very beautiful in white."

Luminescent, she tells you her name is Marie.

At night by the sea, space is vast and smooth. Deep

inside you, hidden beneath the rubble, an image moves and it is no longer you alone. Now you are two on your island, one looking at life, the other at death.

Love is sorrow and happiness touching. It imparts the world's beauty with its dread.

The February wind takes on a wintry sadness. It seems suddenly as if, during the night, life has disappeared into the bottom of the sea. The silence swells. The cities are inhabited by worry, by a wordless truth. The silence continues all over Palestine. The souks are closed. Father, you go through streets, the Orient is losing its voices, it is empty and bare. You no longer see the little caps, the poor beggars, the country people bargaining. A space is disappearing from the world that seems not to want to be remade. It feels like a musical composition without notes or a melody.

Life stops all over Palestine. The strike is a general one, paralyzing people and things. The cities are losing their rituals, becoming backdrops. With troubled eyes you watch the British police force locked doors and requisition all the merchandise. A dead city reveals

apparitions of violence, a refuge no longer, and seems to be disappearing into infinity. You are suddenly afraid of those blind, slowed-down spaces. Jamal al-Husseini's orders are respected. The Palestinian resistance is on the move as it stops the world. The strike lasts one day, two days, three days.

The strike lasts but it does not disabuse you. A breeze blows slowly. The cities pick up again with their noises and mixtures. Then, Father, in lacerating sweetness you find the lost voices and moving images again.

In the old city of Jaffa the winter is mild. At night the streets are deserted, the footsteps of a rare passerby can be heard. There is no sadness in these old, lost neighborhoods, but rather nostalgia for a disappearing world.

A family gathers around a brazier. The house is simple, bright, and clean. Crocheted curtains adorn the windows, an iridescent carpet sheds bright-colored light. It is the living room of the Jaffa potter. He is there, smoking his hookah and playing backgammon with his oldest son. He is a man of few words but it is he who creates the shapes of clay. The mother has eyes as green as the sea. She is strong, she is knitting and talking with her daughters. The grandmother, in a rocking chair, snores as she follows the conversation. The youngest son is studying in his room. One of the

daughters, Martha, is embroidering a tablecloth. The other one, Marie, is pretending to read a magazine. Father, you have just left her, she leads a modest and simple life, but she belongs to you. Her magazine lies open but she is thinking of you. At night she doesn't sleep, she thinks of you, then prays very hard for God to keep you and hide you deep inside her heart. The brazier consumes its ashes, its last glimmers of light. In the distance, the sea is brilliant, dazzling, and the stars are tracing paths of bronze.

Terrorism strews gunpowder and bleeding bodies everywhere. The British want a compromise solution by dividing the region: one province for the Jews and another for the Arabs under their control. Jews and Arabs are dissatisfied. The Irgun kidnaps six English officers; the English then throw hundreds of Jews and Palestinians in jail. The tension is mounting. The Arab League meets. It wants to help the Palestinian farmer keep his land. It makes secret decisions and alerts the West to a possible oil blockade.

During this time, Father, lying on your cot you slowly watch the night pass. Your throat is tight, the wreckage of your past tastes like stale bread. The pale, diaphanous moon strokes your window and slips by. Tomorrow, the most spectacular act of your life will be the attack on Jerusalem's King David Hotel. In this hue of boundless space where the world is born and ends, the new dawn will spread heartbreaking madness. A new sorrow is tearing at you like quicklime — your mother has arrived in Palestine on one of those ships that cross the water like a hard wind. A ghost of herself, her form floats, she moves over the gangway and shatters. You hardly recognize her. She is wearing a bonnet that hides her pain. In Dachau they cut off her long mane of hair.

The night is silent, then suddenly a star bangs against the panes. You find it dazzling and pure and you smile, for your soul has not yet died. Love is Marie tossing white petals like diamond stars.

Dawn rises over Jerusalem in this fluid, liquid light that illuminates and burns.

The streets of Jerusalem are roasting in the July sun. The shade is hot. Children are shooting marbles under the outlines of giant palm trees. At noon eyes blink, the reverberation is so strong that it crackles like a torch. The King David Hotel displays its air of pernicious luxury, of mirrored façades the heat cannot melt away.

In the southern wing, the services of the Secretary General of the English High Commissioner keep important documents found at the Jewish Agency. They had to be unequivocally destroyed before they could be used and the time and memory of others had to be violated to safeguard the secret. The sun is drunken, yellow, and unreal.

Father, your assault unit is approaching. You are dressed like Arab employees of the hotel and setting out pitchers of milk. The whirling heat and the anxiety make your smiles tense and give your pupils a hounded look, yet one of you is singing at the top of his lungs. You can already hear the echo of the bedlam that is to follow.

Near the King David, you divide into two groups. Yours takes the milk pitchers down to the basement, passing the Regency Café. The other group is covering you and your leader is putting notices up announcing the danger, shouting that the hotel is about to blow up.

A smoke bomb explodes. That is how you and your friends find your way out of the hotel. The smoke envelops you in a mirage that fans out, then vanishes. You are outside and have to wait thirty minutes for the detonation. What if the mechanism doesn't work... You have to wait thirty minutes, thirty eternities...

In Jaffa, Marie forgets the city behind her, the sea evaporating in the sun, the deserted piers at noon. She is painting narcissus and roses on her jar. A smell of heat and sweat emerges from the souks. Father, Marie is dreaming. She is following you on changeable roads she imagines to be smooth and far away. Together you stop near a large river, flowing slowly in sacred and graceful silence. You look at your reflections, the water moves and your faces touch.

Marie is painting roses on a jar — a white one for herself and a red one for you. Then she adds countless leaves of green and blue. She smiles, the jar has a fragrance of sweet-smelling petals. Marie sets it down on the shelf. It has to be filled with happiness.

Time moves slowly. At twelve thirty-seven Jerusalem shakes, becomes disembodied, and burns. The explosion is enormous, milk pitchers fly across six floors in a burst of fire, screams, and death. The blaze reduces people and stone to dust. The King David had not been evacuated. Ninety-four people who did not choose to die together are killed. They are English, Jews, Arabs.

The night is blue. Near the glowing cinders, the remains are laid out in rows. Fate has united them one last time, for each one to beg for God's compassion and forgiveness in his prayers. Families weep. Stars fall on Jerusalem.

The days succeed each other, events skid by. The Income Tax building explodes and then the Jerusalem train station. The seasons lurch on, the British police parade around on superb thoroughbred Arabian horses. They are powerless and bothersome to a peaceful population. Apprehension throws people and things into confusion, two of your friends are captured and sentenced to fifteen years in prison. They are given eighteen lashes with the whip. Father, you see them at the moment of the verdict, their ribs showing, their skin tone pallid, their eyes launching a stifled cry. Their faces are stony and pitying. The Irgun is exasperated. A spirit of revenge prolongs things, the world. You kidnap two English officers who are given eighteen lashes with the whip. That night you celebrate this catch in joy and laughter. Your captives have lost their magnificence, their arrogance, and now their faces are ashen with hate-filled, hard lines. But for you, Father, other visions exist and fix a white, transparent figure on a ruffled sea. You retreat and sit down by the side of the water and the waves. Stars and shipwrecks haunt the night.

Images collide over Palestine and give shape to glances fallen deep into the silence. Father, two of your people are hanged and you hang two British officers. A cold fever defaces life and death, life as it stops, death as it takes revenge.

The sun lowers its rays. The river is silent. The mill turns like passing time. It sings of the slow wind. Father, you are with Marie and touch her hand. She throws a pebble in the water, which forms corollas that expand and then break up. She says:

"Look, David, it's like love, it's greater than the wave."

Marie rises, her dress floats around her, she pushes the door of the mill and turns toward you with lowered eyes, because the sun causes her to close her eyelids. The mill is not really dark. The light streams down her face and shoulders. Sitting on the ground, she calls to you and looks at you, broken-hearted. She will never speak a single word of love to you so as not to ruin anything, to keep the immensity of the secret intact.

Father, what a memory of tender feelings! You

come forward and press against Marie. You flatten her mouth, caress her, and put your lips all over her. You want desire to rise, devour, howl. Marie holds you so tightly you could break, she drowns in you like a heavy swell. Blood flows over her. Marie's nakedness is smooth and soft. Her breasts are silky and her belly blonde. You would like to tear yourself away from her but a fragrance of skin and pleasure holds you back, lacerating you. You say:

"Marie, I love you but I no longer belong to myself. I destroy, I kill, and you, you are so pure. My hands are full of blood. I have become a fireball that rolls across the sea without ever being extinguished. Even if I go far away from you, don't forget me. Someone has to love me so I can be forgiven."

Marie's eyes have the look of happiness. They hide bits of mist. She takes your hands in hers, dazzled by you. A halo of half-light surrounds you both like a ring of pink luminescence. Marie belongs to you, her virgin body, her lover's skin, her maternal heart. Right now her gaze is tempered but, underneath, there is her mad affection for you that will grace and age her. In Marie's eyes there is a pure and radiant but very distant light.

The mill turns. Close by the water a bird sings the solitude of the falling night.

Father, I am following you everywhere in your badly written pages. Me, I know nothing of my fate and lay a somber glance on the child I am, on the man who is looking for a name. Always discovering so as to be more real, less futile, and trying to describe oneself in writing. I know now that Marie is my mother. She is a Christian, I guessed that the one time she came to me. Life puts me into her arms but takes her back before I recognize her. I see a cross around her neck that has grown black with time and wretchedness. My emotions are at the farthest edge of all that lives or dies. Father, Marie is a Christian and you love her, I do too and maybe more. Islam venerates her, Christ bleeds for her, she is inscribed on a flaxen page where freedom is equated with love.

Night comes back in its torments and dreams. Coronas of stars are falling everywhere. The night drags, you do not sleep well. At dawn, the muezzins' prayers repeat the same cry of man to God in grave solemnity and eternal hope. The sound echoes from minaret to minaret across the flattened towns, the lost villages, the plains and deserts. From steeple to steeple church bells call people to prayer. All these voices rise in a wind of clouds but vanish and fall in massive savagery. The world waits, sacrificing the present to the past. You, Father, you also wait and search. Events rush on, their memory is immortal and writes the future.

Houses are painted with dust, gunpowder, and blood. Smoke rises like an incense of death. Father, you are impatient, the case of Palestine has finally been taken to the United Nations, which thereby experiences its baptism of fire. An era comes to an end in troublesome visions, the world totters and holds the horror of the camps inside itself. Clouds rush eastward. The United States is in favor of the Jewish State, the Soviet Union is hedging. The world waits, as do you, but your life is transformed into fear, the uncertainty of losing or perhaps of winning.

Elsewhere, in the mountains of Lebanon, in Sofar, fog covers a humid summer evening in gray. The summer sinks away beneath a pale crescent moon. The Arab League has been meeting there for three days. Its members leave the room, their red fezzes, their kaffiyehs uniting them. They refuse to accept a division. The newspaper *Al Ahram* declares there is a risk of war if Palestine is threatened. The world waits, growing impatient. The nights fall in the coolness of an early autumn. The storm is brewing and men no longer contain themselves. The present is compressed, in crisis. England has a premonition of the storm. It announces that it will soon evacuate Palestine.

Father, you write a short sentence in your journal, your hands clenched around your pen. Your handwriting is nervous, uneven, the ink is very dark, but you insist and almost rip the paper: "The British are leaving, now the Palestinians must leave."

And Marie? A scent rises from the soil, a sweet

smell of leaves. You think of her in the depth of silence and bury her far away in your memory. In spite of you, she flows and is inscribed in your flesh like invisible ink. Sirens slash the steel blue of the sky.

Father, the whole world is entangled in your pages. You write and think you are scattering ashes and incense. Weariness clutches and exhausts you. You would like to follow a light wind, heavy with sea, or to wake up somewhere else with Marie in a nebulous and serene light. But through a flora of words the events are scattered and fused. You collect them all in pious devotion. They are recorded in the recesses of your memory, tasting of salt and the beating of your heart as it swells up and dissolves. For you there is no before or after, only a now sealing an eternity, that of a people, a country, and a dream. The General Assembly of the United Nations meets in Flushing Meadow in one of New York's boroughs and votes on the division of old Palestine.

For the Arabs the verdict comes down like a cleaver.

In his gold-embroidered black robe the Emir of Arabia, Faisal ibn Abd al-Aziz, more solemn than the world's oldest patriarchs, turns to Jamal al-Husseini who is representing Palestine. Their eyes meet in misgiving mixed with anger and indignation. In silence they think of the war and those who, in the name of Allah, God, and Yahweh, have died for Jerusalem. The Syrian delegate, Fares al-Khoury, a Christian from Damascus, is thinking of his pilgrimage to Bethlehem. In a voice as dark as an ancient oracle, he says: "The holy places will go through several years of war, and peace will not prevail there for several generations."

For the Jews of Palestine the celebration goes on all night long. They sing and laugh and kiss. In the settlements they pray and bless Yahweh. In your kibbutz, Father, there is a mood of jubilation. You, your friends, and all those who have come from the other end of the world are celebrating the end of the road ecstatically. Father, you run through the streets and dance with passersby, men and women, children with flushed faces, their eyes wide with happiness. What is left of these strong and distinct emotions when they hurtle over into remembrance? For me, Father, this street party robs me of my memory, my childhood, my only remorse.

On the balcony of the Jewish Agency in Jerusalem

a solid woman's silhouette waves its hand. The ungrateful gaze stares at an ungrateful face. It is Golda Meir, the daughter of a carpenter from Kiev, great activist of the Zionist movement. She congratulates the crowd, a hive of activity. This same balcony becomes a temple promontory — Ben Gurion, whose name means son of a lion, always impenetrable, strokes the folds of a huge blue and white flag, bearing the Star of David.

Father, the crowd is milling around you, around the balcony. It is going wild and presses against the piles of stones in the square, the walls. His voice is strong and warm. Enthusiasm is visible on every face, applause blends in, its sound echoing from everywhere. Near you, a figure extricates itself, isolated and distinct, it is a Palestinian with his son on his shoulders. He seems one with the gray cement, snuffed out, but the child applauds because he likes the furor, the shouting, the rays of sun moving around. Father, you never forget the child's green eyes all lit up.

Shock descends on the Arab world but it hounds you because of Marie, her stammering voice, her desire for tenderness. She tells you how the Palestinians almost always live in peace with the Jews and how they have nothing to do with the death camps. She looks up at you with her deep and gentle eyes. The sun is burning you. You know she understands your pain and the pain of your people who in a collective memory seek strength and the making of an imprint. You want to forget her or place her somewhere else at the bottom of a trench to safeguard her. Alone, pale, and smiling she slowly comes back to you with immense white wings.

A truth is haunting time. The anger of the Arab world increases and keeps itself going until the point of exhaustion. Riots burst out in Damascus, Aleppo, and all over. In Cairo, al-Azhar, the great sanctuary of Islamic thought, proclaims the Jihad, the holy war. The land of the Arabs is dismembered and howls like a mother losing her child.

The colors of Oriental nights are thick. You write at night as one scratches basalt or black marble. Writing and finding the strange proof of existence again in order to record a living testimony of an echo, a recollection, an invisible feeling. Writing and your voice going through the night, Father, through time, through the ages. It creates images that history disperses, apprehends, diminishes.

A chalky, sinister fog stains the lights of winter. Minarets chant the prayer at dawn. In Jerusalem, Jaffa, Haifa or anyplace else, a song trembles in the echo and brilliance of the sky. The ulama are ranting at the faithful. They want to cause the eruption of the most relentless war, the war of the streets.

When prayers are done, rioters pour out of the mosques and churches in droves. They shout every slogan they know. With kaffiyehs, fezzes or bare heads, workers, farmers, middle class citizens, women, children, Muslims, Christians, rich and poor form a veritable army of mourning and revolt in the streets. Rioters loot and set fires. The smell is one of smoke clouds and ashes. Flames blaze deep into the night.

The old city empties out. The Palestinian demonstrators abandon it and move on to the large square.

Their ambition has died, they loudly proclaim the world's disgrace. To make sure their shops are spared, Christians and Muslims paint a cross or a crescent on the front.

The sky is blank. In a deserted street a vision of sadness drifts over the locked façades. Father, you are alone and your energy is growing old and dissipating. The city is rigid but weariness dwells inside you. The cobblestone-extended streets are forsaken, as inactivity forces relinquishment. A furtive sound moves and stops, a shadow slips across the walls. You are afraid but it is only a child moving along, with the green eyes of the boy applauding. You watch and wait. He doesn't turn around, the silence reassuring him. He is holding a can of paint, a brush, and draws a cross on a store front. His name is Ali. His parents are demonstrating but he wants to save the shop of his friend Yacoub's father. For years they have been shooting marbles together in this very street. Then, with the innocence of those who never leave childhood, he paints a cross or a crescent on all the stores of his Jewish neighbors. When he has finished his work, he takes a deep breath and smiles. Now he can be sure that he and Yacoub will go on playing with their marbles in their little street.

The towns disappear behind walls of fear. All of a

sudden, Jews, Christians, and Muslims can only be reconciled together in the closed space of cemeteries. Their history is compressed into an alchemy of misfortune that stops only when they escape from the world.

Every Christmas, shepherds of the timeless and the past come back to bring the poor and beautiful child the fairest of lambs. The star of Jesus hides beneath white hope. It is snowing over Palestine. The winter is disconsolate. The flakes are soft and slow.

Father, Marie sits close to you, she is cold and nestles against your shoulder. You say so little but listen to her the whole time:

"Every year we would go to Bethlehem for Christmas, David. The church bells make music. On the square of the shepherds the crowd repeats the same high-pitched hymns that come back down to earth like stars. This year we'll stay in Jaffa since the roads are not safe. Palestine is hurting and in great agony."

It is snowing on the mill, you take Marie in the cold. Outside the snowflakes form glittering petals.

This Christmas is one thousand nine hundred and forty-seven years old. It arrives in snow and white dust. Palestine still waits for the Wise Men and their gifts. The star shines on Bethlehem and only the child in his crib smiles at love.

Father, I am following you everywhere across these turning roads, I would like to have binoculars so that I can see farther than you. You are a doer, a witness. Writing is your loyal accomplice, the sins of war torment you and perish in memory and oblivion. Marie is the one who unnerves and exposes you. Happiness must be paid for, it is memory and dreams.

Elsewhere, in the real world, Jews and Arabs try to stock up on weapons. The Haganah mobilizes men and women and overturns religious conservatism. Rabbis recite the Psalms of David. The youth from the Hebrew University is becoming active. The Gatna is preparing school aged girls and boys for military service. Begin calls for volunteers. He is forming regular units and beginning to manufacture arms. Father, in the Irgun there are now large numbers of you.

In the countryside the Palestinians hold on to their Bedouin traditions. They touch firearms just once, by chance, at a wedding or the birth of a male child. They are loyal and have an affinity for setting ambushes. But they need a good leader, a father—Abdel Kader al-Husseini has that disposition and is close to them. He is a patriot and deeply passionate about the land and tradition. And yet, he is a man of vast and modern culture. He forms the "Jihad al-Mukadass," soldiers of the holy war. In the hills, the men learn to use weapons. The Futuweh is the youth movement. The Palestinians are listening to the radio, the Arab armies promising to come to their aid.

Both sides set ambushes, gunfire sprays sounds of broken stone, red mud, and screams everywhere. The snow is falling. The trees are without leaves, their open arms are frozen. The snow is slow and thick, no one can stop it, slow it down or melt it. Men, women, children are watching. In spite of themselves they are learning to be patient.

One evening, Father, you go through Jaffa. The sea is fog's canvas. Your thoughts are deep and dark. All along the piers the waters are silent. In infinite melodious languor a song by Abdul Wahab escapes from a house. It thrills you and burrows inside you, there where you hide your life. Marie passes through you like a secret and wise conversation.

At the turn where Jaffa joins Tel Aviv, the bars all look alike, one after the other. A girl comes toward you, brazen, sure of her charm, her wares. She is one of those amblers with thick make-up and dead lips that carry a trail of souk aroma and heavy breath. You flee and walk along the sea alone, needing no effort to hear Marie's voice and dream of everything she tells you.

It is cold in the mill. You make love. Marie, sweet and pale, is very tiny against you. After love there are long silences, and then she says to you:

"David, I still tell myself stories before I fall asleep. It is being intimate with my loneliness that keeps it going. Sometimes I borrow these stories from my bashfulness, my desires, and so I give my life a certain autonomy and the stories become so real that I think I may have lived them. You know, David, I tell you all sorts of things, too, and in the morning I wonder if I have been dreaming or if this was before I fell asleep. I believe that this story is really a dream.

"I am in a clearance. The world around me is visible and real, but there is no cohesion. The night is white, magically bright. Four trees around me form the seasons. I don't know which one I prefer, but I like the image of each of them. Suddenly the wind starts to blow. It's not blowing dead leaves or dust around but a stream of stars, the full moon, and a round sun. These constellations are turning in the center of the clearance in a dance of fire. They evaporate as the wind moves. Sometimes, their sparks fall without burning the trees, without tainting the earth and the clearance quivers in the beauty of the morning. I am so very happy and you, David, you are inside me.

"Suddenly, the dance realizes it has natural attributes and takes on the form of a tree, which, in the dream, is a little bit me. The tree puts out roots that join those of the season-trees. The net of roots under my feet doesn't frighten me, it is weaving thick tentacles and then nothing else exists any more. The light is pale.

"You know, David, I think this is the story of the country in which we are born, the country of our childhood, and the roots are stronger than time itself."

"But a strong man puts his roots down everywhere, Marie."

"Listen to the rest of my dream, David. Suddenly, I am dead. Deep in the clearance is my coffin and I am walking behind it. I am both dead and alive at the same time. The roots have disappeared, the season-trees as well. The stars and moon have climbed back up into the sky. The sun has gone down."

You stroke Marie's cheek and smile:

"It's a tale, Marie. You should write and illustrate it."

"I told Mama that I had dreamed I was dead and

she answered that I was going to start a new life. I don't like disruption."

Marie raises huge eyes at you. You lay your hands on her, the mill is turning. She brings you luster, her delicacy, and her simple words alighting from her passion and her dream. They weave a flaxen, bottomless song around you.

You caress Marie, her belly is soft. She quivers, it is me you are touching. You will never know that I exist. For Marie, loving you is your freedom. Night falls in a color of ink and sorrow. The sea etches its never-ending furrows.

Father, you are scattering your life and blowing it to the wind. So many loves tearing you apart! Do you look like those emaciated and tortured men with their ashen gaze contorted by anguish and the world's dream? For me, you are still searching and wandering.

This evening, you go through a small village that is sometimes forgotten and ignored. There, the men cut stone, the women make bread in the bakehouse, and the children play jacks and dream of the future. This spring season is filled with flowers. The almond trees are white or pink. The breeze is delicate and the air is mild. It is a tiny village called Deir Yassin. It is where the road to Jerusalem begins. You stop there and inhale the aromas and sounds. A mad, mellifluous music covers the cicadas' song. This evening no one in the village sleeps. The celebration goes on deep into the night. Silence touches only the stars. It is a wedding.

The assortment of earth-colored houses around you resembles miniatures in which unworldly silhouettes rule over the sonorous dusk with their voices and gestures. Father, you come closer, a woman emerges from the enclosure, the crowd cheers. She displays a sheet stained with blood. The hymen has been broken, love consummated. The wedding is over. The music is unusual, diffused, faded. You walk toward Jerusalem and do not know that the scene you are leaving is entering a night from which it will never emerge. At dawn, the sentry awakens Deir Yassin still drowsy from its wedding.

Jerusalem's sun at noon blinds you. A pink color glosses over the façades and walls, the diluted sorrow created by the expectation of centuries and their posterity. Father, you enter the city of manifold rituals. The Oriental souks draw lively, striking, and indolent passions... the crowd there remains in a perpetual, lavish childhood in which everything can be acquired, touched across the sounds and invisible dust. Jerusalem at noon is a fever, a depletion. The streets are swarming, the British police frisking passersby and sometimes even checking fezzes. You stop in a café, loud music is engulfed by the oppressive air. Some men are smoking hashish, others playing backgammon. The sounds and smells radiate more space than the place actually has. It is hot.

In the back a man stands up and speaks. He is surrounded by Palestinian fighters who are listening to him, revering him. The owner lowers the radio, now inappropriate and superfluous. The man in the back has a sorrowfully passionate look. The words roll from his lips, his romantic charisma makes him wise and paternal. Father, you have just met Abdel Kader, the leader of the Palestinian resistance. Your eyes meet in a shudder and a barely perceptible challenge. For him you are the foreigner to be cast aside.

This leader of men is reporting a story, his voice breaking with anger. He has come from Damascus. Alone, he goes through the streets emptied of their souks. The heat sends off bouquets of light. He reflects upon his interviews with the heads of the Salvation Army located in Damascus, but gets only promises — the ship loaded with arms for which Syria is waiting has just sunk mysteriously in the harbor of Bari. Then, to force the hand of fate and destiny, he buys fifty rifles and three submachine guns with his own money in the souk. He kneels down in the mosque of the Umayyadin and prays for a long time, then visits Saladin's tomb where, with a lump in his throat, he listens to the ghosts of the past. Damascus has the ebullience of gold-dust, an infinite lassitude where the Barada flows. Abdel Kader thinks of his rifles. The Haganah receives cargo loads of arms. Alone in the souks, he remembers all the fighters who battle alongside him for Palestine. Drops of sweat run over his forehead, his eyes cloud over, he knows the men forget themselves in action, bravery, and sacrifice. He walks down the streets of Damascus and hears himself say tonelessly, "Jerusalem, I love you."

The account is finished, the men are surprised and call out. The owner turns up the volume on the radio to cover up the racket but everyone hears, with widespread incredulity, that the Haganah has occupied the village of Castel. The Palestinian fighters are yelling. Abdel Kader calms them down and leaves. A smile of kindness and grief makes him motionless, a fine rain hides his gaze.

At the door of the café a dark-eyed Bedouin woman is throwing her dice. She begs in order to live and have a future and sees one more passerby go out. Then, with trembling lips and feeble breathing, she whispers to herself, to fate: "Death is holding your hand." Father, you slip behind her in the whirlwind of the crowd. Her slow movements attract and frighten you, her irrelevance makes her anonymous. You wish she would throw her dice for you, you would like to touch happiness, desire, Marie, but the Bedouin woman vanishes and disappears into the nebulous hubbub of the streets where shadows and the future grow blurred.

An explosion rouses the world, the silence. The commandos of the Irgun and the Stern gang advance from three directions at once. The sentries of Deir Yassin awaken the sleeping village. Some of the farmers who were celebrating yesterday have weapons, a kitchen knife or perhaps an ax... They defend their women and children with the determination of survival and love.

The attackers converge from every side and find one another in the center of the village where they fall into each other's arms. They are delirious and effusively joyful. But a fever of violence takes hold of them.

David, Father, were you in Deir Yassin? Your silence weighs heavily on you as if your strength, your weakness, could condemn you without your understanding why. To love blood for blood's sake, hate for hate's sake. You must keep your secret, for your face is disappearing behind these black lines. I believe I could never have been that cruel but perhaps life has helped me.

The commandos find one another in the center of the village. They kill. For all who pass by, the fountain flows with dew from heaven, with tears. The dead are tossed into the stone quarry, which creates a legend for yesterday's village. They carry their forgiveness away with them. No one throws a flowering almond branch on their grave, History alone writes them a prayer.

The survivors of Deir Yassin think they are living a bad dream. They will take the road that leads nowhere. They are driven through Jerusalem in trucks, some people spit at them, others feel pity. Deep within they will always, until the end of time, keep the memory of humiliation. Victory sometimes has the savage gestures of shame. In Deir Yassin, despite the vultures circling above the ruins, the commandos come to pick the almond flowers.

Father, the war makes you a lost child. A sense of want gnaws at you, of slipping into the arms of a woman, a mother, a lover so you may endure and forget. A strong premonition keeps you away from Marie, the fear of ruining her, destroying her, but you go back to her. Her speechless mouth calls you in the dark, her voice makes a hole in your stomach. Night brings her back to you when a halo of moon falls over the trees, streets, houses. She sings a lullaby of infinite love to you. Life stops its torment in sleep, forgetfulness, and dreams. Another unreal world opens up in the whiteness of a sleeping town. Sheik al-Tahi returns to you in an extinct cloud of smoke, an imaginary phantom obscured by the night. His voice seems even but gets lost in a bottomless space that is moist and dark. He looks at the swells of the waves, tracks of resplendent and distant lights, and his eyes are warm and sweet, calming. For you he has come across a distant frontier to repeat a story he had told you in Athlit, one long winter's evening. It tells of a desert of arid rocks, savage sun, without any rain or rainbow, a barren soil, solitary and denuded. Its name is the Sinai, perhaps after the god Sin, the god of the moon. That is where Yahweh set fire to a bush and spoke to Moses, close to an azurite stone. In that holy place the Christians built a church dedicated to Saint Catherine. Later, in a handwritten letter, the Prophet Mohammed ordered his Islamic nomads to protect Yahweh's bush as well as the monastery of the Christians, in the name of Allah. Events continue endlessly. Sheik al-Tahi vanishes in the night's rain. He no longer has a face.

Father, a sheik taught you tolerance, a smooth multifaceted way of existing, and you lose yourself by suffering and by trampling on happiness. A sheik took me, your son, your likeness, by the hand to guide me to the very end of violence, to restrain me or expand me. Sometimes, religions wear masks of darkness.

The roads of Palestine lead to the edge of the world. Bluish smoke spirals uncurl in the red dusk. These shadowy, veiled lights unlock the night and extinguish the flaming earth. Father, you are watching the silent shapes of streets and trees, the houses have twisted forms, the village of Castel is becoming familiar to you. It has been four days since you occupied it, you found your friends and light a big fire. The sheep must be roasted to celebrate the victory. Pale flames spread a smell of burning flesh. You encircle the grill and your faces shine with the sweat of heated metal. Springtime lays a mystical glow over the nights. Father, you are watching the stars, they have the secret appeal of mystery, you smile at the night and your face resembles that of the child of Cordouan again, the blond child looking at the waves.

Farther away, another man is watching the same stars, spellbound by their beauty, and inhales the strong scent of the soil, of jasmine. It is Abdel Kader, who loves his Palestine which is his lifeblood, his mother. Darkness shields him and his men. All of them wear combat clothes, the kaffiyehs hide their faces. The night is brilliant, illuminating. Then, in the name of Allah the One God, the Merciful, the Just, they attack Castel.

Father, bewilderment descends upon you, trenchant and paralyzing. You have to fight for three days and three nights, but the village belongs to the Arabs again. The Palestinian flag flies from the tallest house. You lose Castel. Dawn traces a first blue light, but you are all children, punished, betrayed, and disappointed. Joy bursts forth among the Palestinians, laughter blends, but no one knows that the celebration is a funeral rite. They are looking for yesterday's hero but he is lying beneath the rubble. By chance they find a corpse with weeping eyes. It is the body of Abdel Kader. The finest officer of the Palestinian resistance has just died, a martyr of God and the land. With him comes to an end the dream of a tide of drowning men. The hero's cult makes everyone believe he, too, can become a hero. With Abdel Kader dead, the history of a people brings the idol down from its pedestal.

In the Irgun delirium and exultation reign supreme.

Father, you control your gestures and see again the standing silhouette, the face and its features, its gentle radiance. The memory of this man keeps coming back to you endlessly, his voice following an unfinished tale. He leaves the relics of his dreams behind. Life is a hybrid and invites us in the name of freedom to take a place inside cells. It imposes passages on us, collisions, silences. We must understand the unaccomplished. Father, in the distance you hear the lamentations of the Palestinians. Outside, the streets hurl sparks and screams. In a labyrinth of half-light a gray luminescence floats. The anguish of death renders the space sharp-edged and implacable. You go out and the crowd engulfs you.

Abdel Kader, one of Palestine's greatest martyrs, receives the supreme honor of burial beneath the Dome of the Rock. It is a magnificent funeral. The hours go by while the masses moan in grief that slowly joins the silence. As an army of mourning men, women, and children watch over their leader's sleep, his ultimate repose. The coffin is borne covered with the flag of those who fight the holy war. A hurricane of gunfire resounds, then death exacts its end and its respect. Over the esplanade of the Haram al-Sharif hovers, in everyone's memory, the image of a handsome man who will never speak again. Then, in acceptance of fate and destiny, a grieving woman raises her eyes to the dusky sky. Wrapped in huge black veils, she watches the dying light and suddenly her voice rends the air as she cries:

"Allah has abandoned us."

Father, the crowd around you dwindles slowly, an ancient world grows vacant, comes to an end between everything and nothing. What emerges is a barren and deserted square guarding an ode of farewell in gaping remembrance. Marie, her land, your land, love, and death touch and coalesce within you. Suffering is ancient.

This evening of Palestine sweeps away a last season. In the houses haunted by shadows and sadness the poem Abdel Kader wrote to his son before dying is repeated in a fading voice:

> *This land of courageous men*
> *Is the land of our ancestors.*
> *Over this soil*
> *The Jews have no rights whatever.*
> *How could I sleep*
> *When it is in enemy hands?*
> *Something flares inside my heart*
> *It is my homeland calling me.*

Springtime consumes itself in spite of the breeze, the fragrance, and the light.

The Palestinians want to avenge the dead of Deir Yassin but, Father, you and your friends of the Irgun are the ones who everywhere distribute black and white photos of the defunct village. Below the image it says: "If you do not leave, this is what will happen to you."

In the countryside, shepherds hide their herds, flutes, and bells deep inside stables and mills. The declared violence is draining the Palestinians of their courage. They are giving in to fear. And so, in spite of the smell of land, childhood, and ripened grain, they abandon their homes and their past. Long lines of refugees draw slow, black strands in the landscape. Families, looking at the unknown and vast horizon, move ahead on roads of uncertainty and camps. Fleeing, fleeing the land they love, deserting Palestine at sea-drowned dusk to look for dying leaves, nothing but dying leaves in another place. Leaving in a hull bobbing on a donkey's back in a trail of loose stones or perhaps on foot. Walking nowhere to salvage a bit of their memory, their life.

Father, you see that the English are encouraging the exodus. They tell the Palestinians that they will be slaughtered and that waiting trucks are there to save them. From afar, you watch the people piling in like beasts. Sometimes the women are in their nightgowns. They take no objects, no photos, no souvenirs and, in spite of themselves, they obey an unspoken death sentence. Families are not even reunited, they will be scattered over Lebanon, Syria, and Jordan. Father, you think you are relinquishing your will, your victory to forget those whom life wears out, but eyes are opening, opening wide before you. The looks are the same, they contain the silent nostalgia for a forbidden land. You see the Christians cross themselves at every turn. They share the same fate as the Muslims. Faceless, hopeless, they all move onward, walking the land where they were born one last time. They will never forget its fragrance, its incense on the tarnished roads. They move away piously since their land is holy and form columns of silence.

A wind of panic blows across the Arabs. The Palestine Liberation Army suffers the shock of Deir

Yassin as a crushing blow. The circulating photographs proceed like a dance of death. This red dust must cast a new life. The fighters' confidence is shaken, their morale is down. On the road to Jaffa they have lost their artillery. Father, with your friends of the Irgun you capture a train loaded with ammunition that belongs to them. The Haganah conquers cities, towns, and villages. The luck of arms, of the stars shines for Israel.

The streams of emigrants grow larger. Disowned by destiny, they walk on, not knowing they will never return. They draw lines of night foam on the sea and in the land they scrape out furrows of oblivion.

The sea is cloaked in waves. Small boats move away from Palestine's shores. The passengers close their eyes so the sun won't burn them, so they won't see the vanishing land. The Haganah, the Stern, and the Irgun advance their shadows, their armies. The Palestinians leave.

Father, life writes a final page of love for you. You are looking for Marie to save her, to tell her to flee, to forget. At dawn you attack Jaffa... The boats with their refugees dissolve on the Mediterranean.

The night has a fragrance of rising and engulfing tide. It feels as if a world is disappearing in the waters' depths beneath a tepid sky. You walk along the sea, your heart betrays itself. Marie's love is so great, so deep inside you and you didn't know it because life was squandering you in violence. How to lose her? She is a woman who retreats from your arms, an absent figure who will haunt your sojourns and your dreams.

A supernatural, imperceptible light filters through the night. A bewildering devotion leads you to Marie's street, below her darkened window. You wait for her in the night, she will sense your presence. Suddenly the street has the perfume of a beloved woman, of a face bending over you. Marie opens her white crocheted curtain and sees you sitting there, your head in your hands. Between the two of you there is an intangible bond that is infinite and where you are always close, enraptured and vulnerable. Your fingers barely touch, you say:

"You must leave, flee quickly. Tomorrow Jaffa will be attacked."

"Leave to go where, David?"

"Take a fishing boat with your family. Escape by sea…"

"To go where, David? This is my Palestine."

A murmur of passion knocks you against one another. Marie speaks to you, brimming with tears.

"David, take care of me, I want to live with you."

"Forgive me, Marie. Forgive me. I am giving you my journal, perhaps you'll read it, and then you will weep for me. I love you, Marie."

Father, that is how your life comes to a halt, on a

badly written page, with words of love. It continues elsewhere, deep in mystery. Perhaps, before leaving, you kiss Marie's eyes, a kiss of farewell or perhaps you hear her song in a voice of your dreams, your memory:

> *Do not kiss me on my eyes*
> *That would be a farewell kiss.*
> *Kiss me on my lips,*
> *For our words are everlasting.*

Love always has a secret to protect.

The sky is solid blue on the 15th of May 1948. Birds are flying to the sea. It seems to you, Father, you are hearing strange voices, a waltz of unfettered waves. The English are leaving Palestine. You see their ships and vessels melt away in the distance. Black spirals of smoke move off into the sky. A world disappears, another emerges, it is a refuge, a new road for you. The evening before, Ben-Gurion proclaimed the State of Israel. From the Tel Aviv Museum flies the white and blue flag with its Star of David. The shrieking crowd is crushing you. You think you are listening to the primal scream. A whirlwind sweeps you up, dazes you, perhaps you are gladdened and moved, but I, I lose you forever. Far away the sun burns the waves.

Father, here I abandon you and write your life in order to decrease the chasm that separates us. I have never seen your face but imagine it in a crystal ball to carry it away with me. The past, the future, all things sweet and bitter, the words I trace slice into my flesh like a scalpel. Our paths do not cross and I encounter you in the tyranny of the world that guides each one of us to the point of exhaustion. Your life and mine are a dance between two fires, that of good and of evil. How to recognize and differentiate them? We think we are being warmed but the flames are pulverizing. Father, listen to me just once, you and I love the astonishing world of color, flowers, and perfume. We could have been artists, poets, extremes in any case. One day, our sallow faces will shimmer with light, we will look at the world's beauty, for that is of which forgiveness is born.

Father, I forgive you for having lost love, forgive me for having sought it. The heart exists through love, the love we flee, touch, or burn. Without it our lives are delineated in a night darker than night. I abandon you without sadness or resentment and I know now who you are. We are two men who hunt after happiness. One woman, Marie, brings us together in the depth of her tenderness. She is fertile ground in which our roots grow. She offers you her tears, which you forget so you can live, she forgets to smile at me so that I may not die.

Father I encounter and abandon you. I carry you

away with me. My jail is locked but deep inside me I discover a love for you that is profound, insatiable, a white horizon I watch throughout the night. Farewell, Father, we have both lived the meaning of grief and its ravages. Our last prayer is the prayer of forgiveness.

Father, I abandon you for Marie. I have always dreamed of her, of all mothers, of all the ways of gentleness.

Marie, Mother, you come back into my prison, my memory. I read your letter to my father and the memory of you drifts above your fine and even hand-writing. Within these seeping, battered walls your presence is frail and arresting. I see your smooth face again on which lie superimposed the young girl, waiting for love, and the woman who has lost it. The gaze is the same, imbued with dreams... I discover the story of your truth, the one inscribed between the world and you in a sometimes illegible and wordless way. I decipher the lines wherein you hide your freedom, which is failure and bliss, in the dis-possession of your desires. This letter is an immense poem that many women could have written in their loneliness, the sadness of the world's refugees. One evening, you are alone and dare to weep. It is a way of being without destroying that which, within, upsets and escapes you.

Your boat moves away from Jaffa. Every family is pushing to get to a bit of floating wood. It is a world-ending frenzy. With the eyes of memory, every evening, you see the harbor of your city going up in a gigantic conflagration. In the cannon fire flying through the sky, Jaffa disappears in the abyss of waves. It is the boat moving away. Your gaze is riveted on Palestine, but you see nothing any more, nothing but the water. A childhood is torn to shreds inside you and other people are now living in the house. They do not understand the hardy petals on the patio, the well that's dry in summer, the evening butterflies, white at night. They do not know the story of your street and they never hear the voices that resemble all the other voices but that, for you, speak words by which to live and love. Mother, you have left your light deep inside the house. On the condition that others water the roses and jasmine. The sky's boundlessness on your shore, in your city, will remain the same but in your emotions you bear away a passion for your land that will never leave you again. Mother, only love inhabits life, and you, you write to bring happiness out of the fog. Slowly Jaffa disappears in the fog.

Your small boats sail along. The sea is smooth,

motionless, without a breeze. You are going toward Lebanon, others will go to Egypt. At noon, the sun is at its zenith, a thud against heads, eyes, lips, and the water becomes a brilliant mirror reverberating all forms of heat and mist. You are thirsty, there is water all around you but it is salty. You drink salt water. You too, Mother, had to shout for something to drink so that your life can resemble that of David, so that your hearts can meet.

The small boats are swaying on the sea, cutting drifting, somber furrows. Faces are tense, misery is submerged in silence. The reverberation is so harsh that through aching eyelids you can watch the soul of the sea evaporating. A parched old woman falls in the water, wanting to touch the bottom of the waves. The sea takes her away, they retrieve her but she is dead and blue. She has to be thrown back into the water. The swells carry her off. They think they see a pure and lovely young girl swallowed up by foam. A small pink cloud guides her to her eternal home. For you on the boat, she bears the smile, a tradition of Palestine, away with her.

The sun sets. Night spreads, solemn and slow, enormous. Stars are shining. The moon needs the water's immensity. Some people sleep from pure exhaustion, others stay awake and wait. You, Mother, unearth lost images. What renders love greater than its surrounding secret? You preserve David's face inside you, the blue of his eyes, his passion. His voice speaks to you with heartrending sweetness. The love that we do not destroy is always a waiting, an anguish, a memory. In spite of himself, David teaches you patience and impatience. He is inside you and I, his child, belong to him.

The night is motionless. You drift. You are in the boat with your father, your mother, and your sister Martha. Your brothers are elsewhere, there was no more room for them. One day at the other end of the water, the earth, you will perhaps find each other again, but you are a defunct generation. A boat grazes yours with a sharp sound. A woman's limpid voice comes soaring as she sings: "I left my love in Jerusalem." All around, the sea still looks the same. The night is sometimes blue sometimes black, just as in Jaffa. You watch it but it is different, faded. Its voices have diminished. From the distance, the coast of Lebanon can be seen, a thoroughfare. The expanse of land looks like half-light. You wonder if it is real, you think it is huge and empty. The breakers crash onto the shore, touching the unknown.

Your camp is Nahr al-Bared in northern Lebanon. Nahr al-Bared means cold river. All of you arrive on a hill of stones. It is morning, the sun shines on a garden without flowers or fountains. Dogs are barking every-where. There are brown tents for you, straight alley-ways, but nothing is green. It is the land of loneliness. Men become violent, women moan, children watch, their eyes large with fever, fatigue, and fear. A tiny one is crying, he has lost his family and doesn't even know from where he comes. He is barely one year old. The women contemplate these new houses, identical and unsanitary, making dark stains under a harsh light, a cold moon. Here you are all refugees from Palestine. They present you with a bit of hope, but the land is arid, barren, all the greenery scorched. You look ahead, the landscape goes on but the horizon is snuffed out, and an eternity yet to be lived. Eternity is time's frailty.

Mother, you dream of Jaffa, the smell of the sea, the piers in mist, and above all the ever-turning mill. Love needs a hiding-place, a prayer. David lives inside you. In the evening his warmth heats up. At night, in your sleeplessness, you make love. In his absence his pres-ence hurts, lasts, burns. Mother, there is nothing any more, you must forget in order to live a little bit longer. The sun is white and pale.

Inside the camp, life is organized in sorrow. Every day you eat gruel of oats. Sometimes supply trucks arrive. Luxury is a bit of milk and flour. When they are late in coming, children shriek with hunger, the adults do, too. Children rummage through the garbage. The camps are ghettos of humiliation and rage. Fathers turn mean, mothers lose their kindness, and children are rootless. They will be called the children of war, for the land has disappeared, evil exists, and they will never again be able to reject violence. The smoke of the camp rises to the sky, masking the blue air.

Clouds of heat swerve in the sky. They create images, landscapes, flames. Clouds are always nomads, it's beautiful to follow them but then, in droplets, they join the sea. Mother, you watch them and examine the sky for a sign that doesn't come. The waiting drains and destroys, but I am inside you, encircled by your dream. You are still concealing me. No one guesses I am there from the shape of your belly, your loins, your breasts. Fatigue and anxiety have made you thin to better bury your great secret. I am already a thing situated in the night of the world.

In the evening life opens out onto the night. The memory of despair returns to people's faces. Then they all look like blue shadows. Some no longer dare to watch the stars. Then, to stay awake, men tell the same stories — almond trees in bloom, gleaming apple trees, but especially the devastated villages, phantoms of death. You, Mother, look up at the moon. It is full, a mirror of fire. Perhaps David is watching it, too, and you would embrace this way, a moon's caress.

In the summer, the earth is parched, a carpet of brambles and thorns. The sun burns and dies. Summer passes, fall comes early, the winter is rainy and wet. Your sister Martha is getting married. She marries Elias, a boy in the camp who is shiftless and needs a wife. Sometimes people get married without wanting to meet. It is self-destructive but done as a pair. Mother, your love for David is so immense that you have only had time to experience a pale inference of him. Martha and Elias are your opposites but that is easier perhaps, for the world offers them a blessing. Even without love, their children are born of certainty, morals, and life awaits them. Me, I am the son who resembles no other.

Mother, your heart glows with memories. You hear the wind over the sea and you no longer fear time or forgetfulness. A lingering light enters your eyes and again you see the wedding in Jaffa when you tell David your name and hold his look. Already you are crazy about him. You scatter flower petals on his forehead, his dreams, but he is looking elsewhere so that you will follow his face. Here, there is no white gown for Martha. The ululations rip across a heavy autumn sky. You are still eating oat gruel and drinking spring water when it isn't filled with mud. You dare to write only to David that in Martha's eyes nothing is reflected but the brown of tents, the fury of wind and storm. A storm engulfs the camp of Nahr al-Bared. It is Martha's wedding night, it is Martha who is laid to waste.

The storm turns the tents into rags. A downpour of black rain, a frenzied wind deposit a world-ending desolation. Stakes fall, a child dies in the mud. It is the first stormy night, such is life in the camps. The night persists. The following day the light is strange. It trembles in the water drops on the faded leaves. The child is buried, his face white and transparent. A tomb can become a temple. Death is always whole and brutal, but life comes back beyond the storm. The sky is bluish.

In the camp there is a little girl you like. Her name is Basma, which means "smile." Her words are always gentle and sometimes she talks to the wind. This evening, due to the storm, a pole has gashed her head. Blood flows but she doesn't cry. Her lips are pink, her eyes huge with misery. She is alone, you take her into your arms. Your childhood comes back to you, a stormy evening in Jaffa, the sea is black, you are sick. Your mother rocks you and tells you a story to make you smile as you fall asleep: "There is a white queen who comes down from the top of the mountain. Her forehead is banded with a crescent of moon and stars fall from her hands. She comes in the night, smiles at children, and heals their fever and their distress without ever saying a word. She tenderly kisses their eyes."

That night in Jaffa you dream of her and you get well. You tell her legend to Basma. Her eyes have the color of honey and make the light grow larger. Mother, in life there is no white queen, too bad for me and for all children. But tales bring beauty and hope to the world.

In the tent, your mother lays out the mattresses. You are naked and getting ready for bed. She suspects your rounded belly and your full breasts. Then she shrieks and beats her head. Her screams slice into you, she is going to hit you, kill you. There is despair and hatred in her eyes. For her, for them, there is only shame. You have given your body and it is a sin, they do not understand that the body alone is nothing when it is wholly you. And so that nothing will die or be lost, you write to give your purity to David. For the others it no longer exists, they prefer Martha's life.

They put you in the tent. No one is to see you. Shame must be concealed. You are ill, dead, vanished, and cannot live outside because of your belly, because of me, because of the child. Your brothers are not with you. They were never found. They might have understood, unless they are like everyone else. Men write their destiny with their errors and successes. Mother, with David you say you have succeeded in your error. That is a luxury, a dream.

The winter is sorrowful, life sinking into a deep sleep. The air is humid, the cold drifts and slackens time and hope. The sky is unfathomable, tormented and sometimes turns white again. Mother, you are in the tent, it is your home and you think you are entering the unknown from which no one ever emerges. There they keep you enclosed and hide you. It is cold in there. The sounds around you belong to all those who are not alone, to dogs, children, and sometimes birds. Silence follows the sun's crest. Nights are long, dawns pale, days filled, dusk is short. Light is your best companion in loneliness and your letter, Mother, springs from this light. Under the flaps of brown canvas there is a vastness that places a fever, an ache, on you and fades in a shadow of half-open lips. David comes back in the tent and you cannot touch him. Writing him is one way of loving him without making any noise.

The winter is gray. You spend three months in the tent, in the mist, and you wait. Nothing happens, perhaps life happens. One night, there are red shadows around the camp. A cold dankness announces the end of the world. Pain twists your belly. The moment has come. Pale sweat beads on your forehead and makes your hair stick to your temples, your neck, your breasts. You are in such agony, your bones are breaking, your flesh explodes. You are in such agony you are afraid you are dying. To die.

Between two contractions you breathe a little and see a face hover in the night. Secret bonds tear you apart, pain rips you open. Your love requires nothing but comes back consistently in a shudder, it takes shape, moves inside you, and becomes a form, a smell, a voice. You are alone, life gives way, exists. Your mother wakes up and lights the old candle. She gets scissors ready and a tub of water. Your father is doleful, hounded by the secret, the shame. Mother, your head is exploding, you are afraid of dying, dying. Outside the opal moon illuminates the future, the stars are radiant. When your pain stops, the child's cry exposes the night. Mother, I was born from silence and suffering. I am a seeker of breath and tenderness.

Your mother's face has softened, she can smile again, she wipes your forehead and puts me down on your belly. This is a unique and burning nakedness, the very nakedness of love. The candle's flame brings color to your face. Your mother's hands wipe up the dark blood and in a frail and tiny voice she says:

"Marie, it is a boy and it is Christmas."

I was born on Christmas night. The wind rushes the stars. Mother, you hold me tight on your bare skin, your naked heart. All my life I have been the same age, the age of your embrace, a small piece of eternity. Outside the sky is clear and crystalline. Your mother pulls me out of your arms, rolls me up in an old towel, and takes me out into the night. Mother, I abandon you without wanting it, we could have touched golden-spiraled dreams. I, I am a prisoner of fate and you, you flee alone and nowhere do your steps resonate. Bruised, with bare arms and vacant entrails, you leave the tent, the sky is frozen, the stars are cold, the end of the world, of the night, is already there. Milk flows from your breasts. It stains your clothing. No one will ever touch your breasts again.

Shadows describe gigantic and unreal shapes in the shade. The horizon quavers. In the distance the muezzin chants the birthing of the day. Your mother comes back alone, her face calm. She puts her hand on your shoulder and leads you back into the tent. Light draws toward light. The night is ending. The muezzin of the dawn walks to the mosque, where its minaret draws a line of hope. It is he who takes me in, gives me a name from a holy book, his holy book, the Koran. He is right, for I was born from a prayer, the prayer of the world's disinherited.

Mother, you concealed me, and forgotten I must live, I must not exist. I must disappear, die so as to atone for that impossible forbidden love, which in its suffering belongs to each one of us. Mother, I abandon you and your letter makes me weep. You have lost everything and hide your face to live off memories alone. I, the terrorist of Palestine, I want to offer you a verse so you may love life. A day will come when you will emerge from the foam and David will be waiting for you on Jaffa's beach, you will make love, the sea will envelop you, and when I am born, you two will hold me in your arms. That is how we shall live, on the land of promises, to plant the tree of peace and forgiveness.

Father, Mother, your voices come back in stinging ecstasy. I know now that in my violence I hold my salvation, the word of Yahweh, God, and Allah. Your story is mine. Our lives are recorded on different pages, your page, David, which takes the road back, your page, Marie, who searches for me and for you, and then there is I with both of your faces, whose lips are connected by love and torn apart. Provided that time does not disintegrate our pages. My words, and yours, flow in a solitary river to dissolve pain. Our love needs a hiding place, a land, its passion haunts the future.

Mother, you come into my jail with my memories,

a white and distant shadow. You are beautiful and young, and you are picking flowers, life awaits you. A smile brings color to your lips and eyes. You come toward me but suddenly loneliness veils your body and your face. You are beside me here, just once, before I die. I would have liked to paint your face to hide your suffering, to put some light on your cheeks, on your forehead.

Mother, who are to me an unfamiliar face in passing, to you I give my last forbearing smile. You are the heroine of an era that sacrifices one group for another. Time's memory will speak of your pain. You could have been beautiful, amazing, living the fulfillment of love, but your youth perished at the end of an invisible horizon where you are alone, sorrowful, and destitute.

Our tomorrows already belong to History. Again you vanish like one of life's strangers into silvery nights. A fine dry breeze skims over us. The anger inside me has abated, only silence is left. Dawn moves in slowly.

I, Ahmed, the terrorist of Palestine, I find my life and my past again at the very moment that I can no longer touch them. The acts of war and oblivion change the course of my story and it is through irony or a certainty of hope that I, Ahmed, direct myself to David and Marie. My syllables are newly found, uncertain, but they bring you, Father and Mother, together so that your wandering words of tenderness can finally touch and grow old together. I, your son, have lived without you, in a desert drained by the winds, and I have dreamed of drowning my soul at the bottom of wild waters to find an island, a city, to find your image.

My life comes to an end within gray walls, discolored by time and torment. There is a taste of blood in my throat, the same taste of sap that runs deep down inside a tree. I open my arms wide like branches, they hurt so much. My breath is coming more heavily, the torture has consumed my body and my dream. Father, Mother, I need your love so I can die, I am waiting for your forgiving gentleness.

I hear the wind dancing in the leaves of the olive tree, the sea running along the shores like an accomplice of beauty, the sun setting in its stately flames. Now I love every color of the light. I am touching the last bands of light penetrating my cell. I make shadow figures, that is the story of my life.

I am a terrorist, a dreamer. I have removed my mask of bliss for that of fear and sweat. I have lost. Some call me a hero, others curse me, but I have chosen my own image, my own identity, for I was soft wax that had to harden, inexorably.

The night is falling, tinged with cinders and incense.

Stars begin to shine. The shadow covers me with thoughts of peace. I bow down. It is the deepest prostration before God because I, Ahmed, am the son of David and Marie.

∪